THE
SNAKE
HANDLER

by
Cody Goodfellow
and
J David Osborne

BROKEN RIVER BOOKS
EL PASO, TX

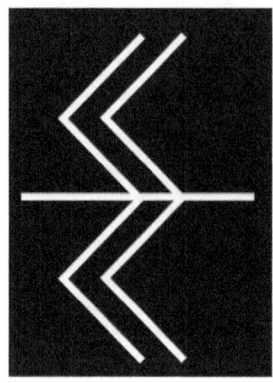

A Broken River Books original

Broken River Books
Parts Unkown
El Paso, TX

ISBN: 978-1-940885-39-1

Printed in the USA.

for
Harry Crews

And these signs shall follow them that believe: In my name shall they cast out devils; they shall speak with new tongues. They shall take up serpents; and if they drink any deadly thing, it shall not hurt them; they shall lay hands on the sick, and they shall recover.

—Mark 16: 17-18

1

It bites me.

My right hand deep in the rusty mailbox, clutched around a big parcel crammed in tight like our postman Dale never would, and like the dumb monkey with its hand stuck in the jar, I'm too stupid to let it go. Scales like blackberry thorns brush my knuckles and they know what I'm touching faster than I do. The parcel comes loose and I jerk my hand back, but I'm bit and the rattler comes halfway out the box with its fangs in the meat between my thumb and index finger.

I'm going into shock before I can blink. I know what to do, but it's not me that grabs it behind the head and draws it out so the fangs retract or flings it back in the mailbox and slams the lid.

You know right off when you get a bad dose. How could you not? That old sick weedkiller-moonshine rush balloons up out of the twin syringes pumping into

1

your veins and pops the top off your skull, and you know nothing else. From the depth and spread of the bite and volume and potency of the venom, you can tell it's a big old tom rattler, startled by a warm hand in that cold box.

I know that bite of old. I learned to love it before my first sip of whiskey. But like a surprise party in prison, seeing your first crush working the pole or a bump of good glassy crank tucked in a hymnal, just wrong, all tangled up and throwing off sparks of haywire impulses.

All I can think is, *I didn't hear no rattle.*

I demonstrate my faith more nights than not, and as often as not, I've been bit. But I'm out at the end of my rutted dirt drive in a old bathrobe and flannel pajama bottoms and a yellowed undershirt still clammy from the night sweats, and I wasn't ready, couldn't warm up. The morning dew makes jeweled miracles of all the roadside debris. Trucker bombs, amber and ruby taillight debris, cigarette butts and dogshit and honeysuckle.

I go limp like to fall back into your arms, but nobody catches me. The earth opens up and the sky turns to dirt and I fly up the ladder of fire racing up my arm.

Fly up into the mouth of clouds, the tunnel of light beckoning and I'm soaring into it, watching the world shrink and shrivel into a ball, then a blue speck, and the light grows so bright, I can't make out the smiling faces peering out of the clouds, but my heart sputters with awe as I recall faces from history books and faces older than photographs that I know by heart from the Bible, and all are looking on me like I'm the one holding the key, like my hand knocking on the door will open the gates at last and all will come to jubilee and judgment on my coattails.

At the end of the tunnel, where the light is too bright to make out what lies beyond, something reaches up and drags me down. I fight but I can't resist, and then I stop trying.

I'm surrounded by my father, grandfather, and great-grandfather, standing on a cliff of curdled clouds beside a rushing river of souls. Daddy wears the suit he was buried in and the crude prosthetic hook they swapped for his hand in Vietnam. Granddaddy wears the overcoat he wore when he disappeared, his pockets still bulging with rocks, his head gnawed down to a nub by catfish and buckshot. His father holds the hand-carved cherrywood box of rattlers he used to stick his hands into, the ones that bit him to death. It rasps and clatters when he shakes it.

My heart sings. I have so much to ask them. Daddy takes my hand and says, *Son, you finally made it. Thought for a second you were gone fly right into the light with all them damn rubes...*

I look up at thousands of firefly sparks sucked into

that greedy glow, see them flare and flicker out like gnats in a bug zapper. No wings, no halos, no harps. Their ashes rain down on us like gray snowflakes to catch and dissolve on Grandaddy's exposed, panting tongue.

I'm ready, I tell them, *Let's go on to Glory*, and that makes them laugh.

This is all there is, Daddy says, *and this much only because we made it out of faith*. He takes my hand tight and holds it like I'm about to be baptized. *It's a good racket, boy, and you fleeced 'em as good as any of us.*

It ain't all *there is*, Great-Granddaddy says, dropping his snake-box so a mess of shed skins and severed rattles spills out. *There's the old goddamn thirst*. He takes my other hand.

I feel agony like nails coming out of my palms. Little mouths in the hollow of each hand weep copper venom. *Not a drop of blood in him*, Daddy says as he helps his faceless father find my hand and he laps the sweet nectar from my stigmata.

Great-Granddaddy falls to his knees and digs his fingers into the spear-wound in my side. *You died right, Boy*, he says. *We're real proud of you*. He presses slobbering lips to a gusher of venom and cries like a drunken baby as he sucks me dry.

* * *

The cold of the earth in my joints and the piss pooling under my ass pull me up off the roadside. I wipe my head and the pain in my right hand nearly puts me away. Head swimming, seasick. I lever myself up to see into the mailbox and the glint off an eye like a copper finishing nail. I slap the tin lid shut and stumble up the drive, holding my swollen right hand under my left because every jolt makes me fit to puke.

Thank the Lord my wife isn't in the bathroom. I sit sidesaddle on the toilet, breaking one of the bolts holding the seat on. I drag out a first aid kit from under the sink. I press the suction tool over the wound on the back of my hand and squeeze the bulb. The blood that comes out is almost orange. I don't know how long I was unconscious, it could be too late, I should go to the clinic and get a course of antivenin…

I close my eyes. *If you will it, Lord*—

A cold numbness creeps over my scalp and down my spine, but my heart keeps beating, my left hand is steady, and a little voice tells me my soul is so black and bloated with sin that the venom might as well be milk, and hell will seem like heaven, if I ever get there.

2

Dear Lord,

After fifty-two years in this world, I can only conclude that you just haven't been paying real close attention. And I know we haven't had much occasion to speak— at least, I've gotten used to getting no answer—but I know you won't hesitate to judge.

So I have to get my shit together.

I wrap the punctures in gauze and tape it down. Already the swelling in my fingers, and that familiar asthma in my chest, like snakes around my lungs. The house shifts and settles but otherwise keeps its stillness.

I take stock of my surroundings. When you're fucked up on venom, the best thing to do is quickly ground yourself in the familiar. That means the old crayon drawings gone yellow at the edges magnetized to the fridge and I can smell the iron rust and wax bonding together there as they had been over years. The rubber faces of the magnets—Spock, Precious Moments, Garfield, a map of Texas, Jesus, Tony Robbins, Dilbert.

The top of the fridge lined with boxes of oatmeal and cereal and coffee grounds gone to a thick paste from spilled corn oil I never cleaned up even though the Clorox wipes are right there next to it, towering above the small bottles of aspirin and gummy vitamins and Benadryl, a few of those spilled out across the stove crusted thick with tomato sauce and tiny macaroni noodles never cooked laying in chicken-feet patterns across to the sink thankfully, blessedly empty of dishes but still in need of a wash, and at that sink I turn on the tap and let the water get good and cold and I cup a good amount in my hands and I can think again, I can see my daddy and his daddy and his the way I've always seen them, before they saw me from where they saw me.

I turn the tap off and look out over the bar to the living room, the yellow couch Sally's dad left for her after he died, and the faded pink rug with white fringe uncoiling, nothing in the fireplace but old dust, the mantle stocked with what I remember just fine and a Big Mouth Billy Bass thirteen years deep into a vow of silence. I sit on the couch and wait for Sally to wake up.

She comes out after the sun, not even looking at me, straight to the coffee machine. I hear the wooden click and creak of cabinets opening, shuffling of plastic, the stiff rustle of filters, grounds poured. I smell the coffee mixing with my sweat and the gurgle of the pot could be my lungs laboring up and down, the hiss either my breath or the machine or the devil gotten into me through two small wounds.

She sits down cradling her mug and doesn't speak until she's had a few sips.

She sees the bandage and doesn't even ask.

"Looks like this one got you good," she says.

I clear my throat. "Probably it did."

Sally settles the coffee mug in her lap and fixes her gaze. "Should I call Alex about the yard, or do you think you might work through it?"

I look down and my hand is a crab claw. The gauze turned black and thick, rubber bands keeping my claws tight and I'm behind glass tapping it, impotent and ready for a hand to come down and pick me up.

I blink. "I can do it."

Sally smiles big. "Look at us. You cut the grass, I'm in my garden. We got old."

Not a hint of worry on her face. She's seen me go through this before. At first it bothered her a bit, understandable considering. Straight out of high school and drunk as hell at the big Elizabeth game on a clear, cold afternoon, reliving a time maybe, holding on to it for as long as she could before it was gone forever. I made her laugh and let her drink out of my beer hat, and soon we got dinner together.

I stumble to my workshed. Shut and bolt the door and slide the workbench away from the wall, working painfully slow, cradling my stricken hand. The false wall was originally built by my great-grandaddy to hide the snakes and other articles of our peculiar services from the hardshell southern Baptist sheriff at the time, though West Virginia was the only state that never outlawed our practices. It's been long since forgotten by all but my uncle Huey, Lee Sweet and myself. My granddaddy may have made use of it to hide corn liquor from time to time.

The storage space behind the wall contains nine pounds of vacuum-sealed marijuana, two of crystal meth and a couple ounces of pharmaceutical-grade cocaine; a couple thousand pills, including Oxys, Vicodin, Viagra, Valium, psilocybin, and thirty flavors of amphetamine; a pair of cut-down pump shotguns and a beat-up brown leather briefcase with thirty-five thousand dollars and a police revolver in it. I take the briefcase and put everything back, then stagger out to my truck.

3

When I was three, I drank a bottle of formaldehyde. Wasn't witnessing or trying to impress anyone, but Daddy said you were always watching.

Toddling around in the dooryard of my daddy's place, one time after Mama went back with her own folks. I remember his big Great Danes herding me around like a fat little sheep. I remember being thirsty and seeing Daddy drink out of brown glass bottles and give me a taste when his new girlfriend wasn't looking, and I found one in the shed where he used to dry marijuana, and I drank it down.

I remember burning from the inside out. My breath came out like the heat haze above a fire. I staggered into the kitchen to beg for a glass of milk. Daddy's girl was from the church and he was afraid the girl's father would come after him, so he and my uncle were sitting on the front porch with a shotgun close by.

When he smelled my breath, he lifted me up and began to speak in tongues. The girl brought the milk out in a mayonnaise jar but he knocked it out her hand so the milk and glass and blood from her hand dappled the screen door until the dogs licked it off.

The poison turned my insides to fire. I tried to sick it up, but he pinched my lips shut and prayed over me. The neighbors came running and put their hands on me and I floated up and they were not lifting me but reaching out to keep me from floating up to heaven like Elijah, and Daddy sent that girl back to her family and reopened the church and witnessed that he was a new Abraham, that God had taken his only son to awaken his faith, and returned him to spread the Gospel. He kept me with him after that, because I had shown myself a prophet.

Know what you're thinking.

Like, what would a gent who gets off being bit by snakes to prove the strength of his faith need an antidote for?

We hold you above all earthly things, but sometimes I wonder if even you have any clue why we do what we do. Maybe you think we all fuck our cousins and lynch niggers and brew white lightning in pointy-headed white sheets, and we're so daffy with the blacklung and the love of a long-gone God that we get up to shit that would shame a jungle witch-doctor when we witness to your power.

Sometimes, it's who and what we are, and sometimes, it's just when we know you're looking, because we know you hate us like you must secretly hate yourself.

I've taken up serpents and drunk poisons when the Holy Spirit moved me in services, and I've witnessed at home when I felt myself tried or tempted. We get bit fairly regular, and it does not shake our faith. We *know* we'll get bit, and we know from hard experience that we may take sick and die. We ain't saying we're so special the Lord drops his business to keep us safe. We're falling back into His arms to demonstrate that if He doesn't see fit to catch us, we're just as happy to go where we're sent next.

But there's always a trick to it, ain't there? That fancy underpants wrestling they got on TV is fake, but they still get hurt now and again, and folks still pay to see. I've never been to a Catholic mass, but I'm pretty sure those crackers and grape juice they serve ain't anybody's body or blood.

I've known preachers who milked their snakes before every service, so the bites were little more than dramatic beestings. My Daddy guzzled a jelly jar of foamy death every Sunday and told his flock it was strychnine and battery acid. One night, he gagged and dropped dead at the pulpit, but all they found when they pumped his stomach was Mountain Dew and apple cider vinegar. Folks said it wasn't you, but the sheer power of his faith that he was drinking poison, that struck him down.

Yes, belief is a powerful thing, and I can well understand why it's your drug of choice. Sometimes, I suspect our belief is all that holds you together, and floods, fire, famine and war follow whenever you're aching for a fix.

Our faith is no more a magic trick than it is backwoods stupidity. We have no lack of trials and hanging judges here. Life is a test most fail before they're born, but we demonstrate our faith that the Lord is something more to us than a cheerleader for the better job or bigger truck.

It'd be a hell of a way for someone to put me down. *Ol' Clyde got himself a taste for the bite, and he fixed up at home before his morning coffee, and just like all those longhaired musicians a couple generations back, he shot up out of turn and just nodded off—*

One thing makes snakebites like heroin: you get fixed in one place and it grows on you, feels safe, but then you take the needle in another place, same dose, same needle, even, and it hits like ball lightning and knocks you dead. Sometimes the spirit moves you, and sometimes, you need to have the antidote handy.

All this running through my head as I drive into town, my good hand on the wheel and the other like a sick dog in my lap, the briefcase on the seat beside me, the rattler in a canvas drawstring sack in the passenger footwell.

Someone put that snake in my box. I make a mental list of everyone I can think of with the motive, means, and big brass balls to try me like this. And I'm in luck, because I'm meeting most every one of them today.

I follow the road down Two Run Creek and turn onto Palestine Road, take it north into town. Looking in my rearview, I take out my phone. I hit the contact for the church.

"Holiness Pentacostal Church of God With Signs Following," says a stern voice I have to recollect myself to recognize.

"Hey, Enola."

"Hey, Reverend. Why ain't you coming around church in the morning anymore?"

"Darlin', last night's service lifted me clean out of my shoes. Dang near four hours. But maybe if you baked another of your rhubarb pies..."

Enola chuckles. "You know your wife would birch your hide if she knew you tried any other woman's pie."

"She uses too much sugar."

"Then how come mine's the sweetest?"

"Darlin', you don't need to use *any* sugar. Now, is Huey around? Lemme talk at him a minute, would you, dear?"

She flutters away and by and by, my uncle Huey picks up. He says nothing, but you can tell he's there. It's a big sound, like a river breathing.

"You hear or see anything in the way of a message this morning?"

He shrugs. It sounds like a distant mineshaft caving in.

"Anything from the angels yet?"

He shakes his head, which has its own weather.

"I got errands to take care of. How much is in the collection basket?"

Tongue clicking against teeth like a rabbit teasing a beartrap.

Nothing. None of our retailers dropped anything in the clothing poorbox out in the parking lot so far today. So far, Lorna Gunn hasn't answered any of my texts.

I thank him and remind him to see about the snakes. Take a careful count, but I already know this rattler wasn't one of ours.

I hang up and look at the canvas bag slowly squirming in the cold blue shadows at my feet.

Eastern diamondback rattler. A big sonofabitch, just over two feet and thick as my forearm but still young, so it can't strike without emptying its young, dumb glands into the victim. Somebody cut its rattle off, which drove it mad with agony and made it a weapon.

Our snakes tend to be old and sickly. We ain't cruel

for the sake of cruelty, but the snakes we take up are kept in dark boxes and fed as little as we can get away with. This keeps them docile and weakens their venom, even if they strike. We go through snakes faster than socks.

Garth wants to show me something on his phone.

Hair clipped down to nicked scalp on the sides and slicked back with greasy kid stuff on top, highlighting bad dandruff, jug ears, sloping brow and weak chin retreating from a formidable nose. His bulging, uneven muscles look as natural on him as the European fatigue jacket and capped teeth, or the arcane tattoos peeking out the cuffs and collar of his silver shirt—numbers and bar codes, so when he waves his arms at the Walmart checkout, a swastika and a passage from *Mein Kampf* show up on the scanner. But Garth is nonetheless a warrior.

After bitching about the bandwidth at the diner, he finally gets this video to play. Makes me watch the whole thing.

I drag out getting my glasses long as I can, but still see burning people spill out of a column of trucks like ants deserting a picnic.

"Wait for it," he says.

The big truck in the front explodes and a lady on fire throws something to a man in the road just before the video freezes.

"Suck on this, goofers!" Garth laughs and slurps his milkshake. "Luckiest little hadji in all of the Stans. All our shiftless dindus could take a page from that book…"

When he's not popularizing innovative new racial slurs, Garth runs the computers for a security contractor that works with the Pentagon, so he gets sneak previews like this often. Sometimes it's green night-vision sex videos of folks who're big shit on TV or Snaptweet, or whatever. Most of the time it's brown people on fire. Garth Stromberg is my window on the world.

"You do that?" I ask.

"Fuck, I wish… Guy who did is one of us, though. Know him through some drone usergroups on Stormfront. But it won't be long now…"

Garth grew up two towns over, but hardly has any accent. Took special courses they sell to people who want to go on TV news. "You see so much defeatist agitprop on the cable and the web, it seems like they'd throw on something inspiring like this to show we're still getting shit done in the world. But I know it's not the media's place to put people at ease, and God bless 'em for that."

"I doubt if God has any blessings for the folks who

do the news. The whole Internet is one big golden calf…"

"It knows all, sees all, answers prayers and judges and damns you. You should love the Internet, Clyde. Hallelujah, God is finally real!" He laughs and forks up the last of his syrup-soggy toast. Little sticker on the menu still covers the word "French." The ink wore off a decade ago, but most folks around here still call it Freedom Toast.

"But that isn't why I'm here," he says. "I've got this setup at home, a teledildonics rig linked to a Fleshlight buried in this Real Doll. It's fucking fantastic. I print out different faces for the doll. Did Chris Hemsworth the other day. Imagine Thor with bigass titties sucking your dick through his pussy. Just imagine. What a time to be alive! It's about as close to the real thing as you could imagine, but still leaves much to be desired. Hard to explain, I guess. So here I am, risking my venereal health to score some rare backwoods poontang."

"I wouldn't know…"

"They got this trick where they lobotomize them, no shit. Just drill a hole in the slut's forehead, and they implant this joy buzzer in there so when you're balls-deep and you hit this button, it's like a fucking afterburner, Clyde. They start shaking and jolting, and it's like you stuck your dick in a lightsocket, and you win a T-shirt if you can stay on the whole eight seconds."

All the shit he's fed me every time I've had to meet him, and I still can't tell if he's just making it up to push me off-balance before he gives me the real needle. "Go fuck yourself. Ain't no such thing."

"Hey, don't knock it, preacher. A fuck machine with a piston stroke speed of 1.2 inches and the face of an Avenger has nothing on a wet braindead bitch with an on/off switch. Finally got something out here to attract some tourism, you should be thrilled. All the mines are fucked, so put the wives and daughters to work. Dynamite the shafts and start drilling holes. Be the Bangkok of the Appalachians, for real."

Should go without saying by now, but I wouldn't be eating breakfast with Garth on this or any other morning, if I wasn't under his thumb for seventy-five grand.

"But you know why I'm *really* here. In my least favorite capacity. I'm your fucking *tech support*, dawg. Because it seems you're still not familiar with the direct deposit function on our shared account. Just point and click that shit, bitch. You're not even servicing the principal on your loan, and when I gently touch you about it digitally, you finally seem to be aware of how to hit the Reply button, but I can't make heads or tails of what you're typing, granddad." He reaches over and spears the last of a fried egg and dips it in gravy, then eats it. "Maybe you should try unplugging it and rebooting your operating system. And I don't mean your fucking computer."

I concentrate on my breath, on the sickly swelling of my right hand, of every atom of air between us like a million billion tiny, ticking alarm clocks. When I forcibly unclench my fist, all the blood in my body floods into it and I feel about a single, solitary unkind word from bursting like a black balloon. "I've been more than straight with you. We made some decisions that didn't pan out…"

"No shit. You planned for *this*, but *that* happened." Stabbing every point of this lecture with his dripping fork. "It's not insured. It's the only free market left, and even that's shrinking. You're heavily invested in weed just as they're legalizing it to pacify the urban scum, so it'll be big pharma growing it, not you. You set up to cook crank for miners and truckers to keep up with jobs they don't have, anymore, and you dragged your feet and missed the opiate train. All the White Man has got left is pain, and all he wants is to float above it. Tough shit. It hurts, I know. Take the blue pill and forget it, dawg."

He sets his fork down, still chewing, breathes heavy out his nose. "But you're still into us for a lot more than you'll ever be worth. And we're not pointy-headed rednecks in sheets. I represent a whole mess of powerful, connected folks who'd rather invest their capital in the Cause than in the Jews' sucker-bait casinos on Wall Street. They believe in the perpetuation of the White Man, and they want to see him living and worshiping free, working and breeding and buying on credit forever and ever, amen. But this shit ain't tax-deductible, and it sure as shit ain't charity."

I push the briefcase across the floor until it stands between his patent leather boots. "Take it. I'm well shut of it."

The little plucked Hitler mustaches of his eyebrows go halfway up his forehead. "You're *what*?"

"I'm out. It ain't all there, but I'll get you the rest directly—"

"Not good enough, Clyde. Here you're telling the bank you're quitting your only paying job..." He shakes his head and mouths the word *Out* again wonderingly as he pulls the briefcase up on his knees under the table. He dicks around for a moment with the combination lock I never bothered to program, then pops the latches.

He looks down into it for a long minute, then back up at me with no expression whatsoever before closing it and putting it back on the floor. "Is this some kind of hillbilly declaration of war?"

"What do you mean?"

"Did I fucking stutter? I gave you *money*. What the fuck is *this* shit?" He kicks the briefcase into my knee.

"I told you, I'm out. I'll have the rest…"

"The *rest*?"

"In a week…"

"If I give you a week, you'll give me another free reacharound, but unless the mines reopen tomorrow and crank comes back in style, I'm pretty sure we'll be having this conversation all over again, except with fewer excuses and more visual aids."

He pulls up something else on his phone. "I'm particularly fond of this one." More drone footage: the target spears out of full night blackness, a white spire, with a cross atop it.

"This one oysterlips church was the only polling place in the county that went for that muffdiving cuck bitch last year," he says.

As the church zooms closer, white trails fan out from the drone like bottlerockets. Stained glass windows blow out and flowers of fire bloom up among the pews.

"That one *is* one of mine," he says, sliding out of the booth. "Suck on *that*."

I sit there for a while, watching him get in his hatchback and peel out of the lot.

I take out my phone and clumsily peck out a text to Donna to see if she's at the clinic. No answer.

I slide out of the booth, nearly tripping over the briefcase, foolishly lever myself up with my right hand. It's like pushing a plunger that flushes death throughout my body. I start to swoon, clawing at the empty plates and sweeping them off the floor and everyone is looking at me.

"Hey, Reverend, let me help you," someone says, and I can't recall his face or his name for a scary moment, but I take his arm.

"You look like ninety miles of rough road," he says, and then I recognize Rod Kelcher, who used to manage the drugstore until it went away. He's still one of mine. His people were among my great-granddaddy's staunchest backers when he first turned from his old, bad ways and began witnessing in tongues and taking up snakes. Rod and his wife and two sons sit in the front pew every Sunday and Wednesday night, when he hasn't been beating them.

"I'm praying on it," I tell him, and he offers to drive me home, but I pass it off as just a spell I had after a big breakfast, hoping he didn't notice none of the plates are mine.

He nods solemnly. "Lord lift you up, brother." Rod's daddy, mad with grief over his dead mother, went blind from drinking poison. Nobody in the circle judges the faith of one who takes ill from witnessing, but it was pretty clear at the end Jed Kelcher wasn't seeking salvation.

He follows me out to my truck. "We're real grateful for your sermons, Brother Clyde. My wife, especially, she's been in an awful way since I lost the old job… She rides me and rides me about it, sometimes I can't get a word in edgewise without taking her in hand… but I got a new one—"

I tell Rod that's mighty nice, and congratulate him. He nods, but clearly he's got more on his mind.

"So like I said, I got work, but I'd rather… Well, I heard a couple boys talking, and… I got a chemistry degree… If you ever needed, you know, another hand in the kitchen…"

Rod takes my keys and opens the truck door for me, sets my briefcase on the passenger seat. He leans on the doorpost to help me up. I grab the door and slam it shut on his fingers.

He screams high and hard, but nobody else hears. Jimmy Meacham drives by in his truck and turns into the lumberyard gate behind Massie's True Value Hardware. He waves and I wave back.

I lean in close so he can see me through the red fog of pain I know is clouding his mind. "I ain't your brother, Rod Kelcher. I'm your shepherd, do you understand me?"

He couldn't understand any less if I was speaking to him in ancient Babylonian, but he nods, clutching his mangled hand to his chest.

"And if you never see me again, know that I will still reach up and drag you down to hell alongside me if ever you lay a hand on your wife or children again, do you understand me?"

Rod steps back, head bowed, shaking, and I see he's pissed himself a little. I feel bad, but I have no time to show him forgiveness. I've looked away too long, and I have so much sin to eat, and my time is so very short...

I look at the briefcase for a long time, half-expecting it to start thrashing around like the bag. If the snake didn't do the job, maybe this one is filled with anthrax or scorpions. Only thing I can say for sure I won't find in there, is thirty-five thousand dollars. I close my eyes and think, *You and me, Lord*, before I finally pop the latches with my left hand and flip it open.

The loose wrapping is layer upon layer of shed snakeskins. Inside it is a spill of grimy brass and white like tiny bones: cheaply minted company scrip from the old Axton Mining Company that used to run Kanahwa County, paid to miners instead of cash to spend in the company store; and a bunch of little white pills with a batch number stamped into them.

160 MG. I don't need a pharmacist to tell me what they are. Oxycontin pills of a dosage so strong, the company discontinued it. I think long and hard about taking one or more, or all of them,

but I shut the suitcase and push it down under the seat.

I'm going to need the pain, where I'm going.

4

Palestine is four short blocks on the Palestine Road, beside the Little Kanahwa River. Most of the shops are empty or converted to cheap apartments and storage, but we still have two bars, a liquor store, a hardware store, an auto and tractor parts shop, a couple antique and craft shops, two post offices since nobody here likes the federal one, a medical clinic, a seven-room hotel with a halfway decent diner and an Exxon station. Anyone wants to eat or shop fancy, there's a Hardee's and a Walmart in Elizabeth, the county seat, four miles away.

In the Depression, half the town sold shine and corn liquor to the other half and to the miners up the road in Elizabeth, which earned us the bad reputation we now wear with lopsided pride. Now, half the town is unemployed or lost their own land, almost as many are on some sort of disability or government aid, and the biggest job growth is in defrauding Medicaid and selling Oxycontin. Every shopowner who's still afloat jokes about opening a church with a drive-thru pharmacy.

Some gray rain leaks out of tarnished silver clouds. The wornout wipers smear little crumbs of black, rotten rubber all over the windshield, the blades squealing with every pass.

After the diner, I go down to Enterprise Road and pass the urgent care clinic. When I don't see Donna's old Toyota out front, I go down Smith and park behind the abandoned chain drugstore. Place next to it was a Montgomery Ward catalog shop until the 80's; then it was Molly's Attic, a thrift store and a seamstress until Molly Cykes died four years back, and then it was nothing.

Last year, a Halloween store opened for two months, and all the faded orange signs are still up. The lights are on this year, and you can hear machines going inside like they're renovating something fierce, but Halloween came and went, and they never opened their doors.

Scan the radio—tinshit "young country" by metrosexual Australians, "classic" rock from long after rock died, and a call-in show with Lonnie Dove, that minister over in Elizabeth. The announcer reminds you not to call in, this is a replay of the Sunday afternoon show, but he'll be live again tonight, as every night.

A woman calls in blubbering that her man won't stop jerking off to the internet. I turn it off.

Looking at my hand, I go over Garth. He enjoyed putting the blocks to me too much to be surprised I was still alive. I'm the daddy he never had the guts to kick around. Without me, he ain't getting his seed money back, and if he took it, he couldn't keep from crowing about it for long. But it wouldn't exercise him none if somebody else tried to kill me this morning. If I die, he'll be showing his church-burning videos to my wife at the wake.

Anyone could've put that snake in the mail, but only Lee, Huey and I know about the storage cache in my workshed, and I trust them two a good sight more than I trust myself. And therein lies the problem…

I take a tall sip from a jar of stomach tonic from under the seat, let the sickening burn go to war with the blackness in my blood for a few minutes, and when I'm sure I won't throw up, I get out and go knock on the back door of the Halloween store.

The screaming power tools all shut down and the door opens up on the second knock. A Mexican bigger than the door stands just inside. Wearing a big black Stetson, a richly embroidered cowboy shirt and new black jeans with a gold hubcap for a beltbuckle, snakeskin boots.

Cody Goodfellow & J David Osborne

He tucks a gold-plated automatic in the back of his belt and pulls me close for an expert patting down and heartfelt hug. "Padre Clyde! So good to see you! But you really shouldn't be seen here. Come in, you know, regardless…"

I tell Angel it's good to see him, too. He ushers me through a stockroom filled with boxes of everything but Halloween paraphernalia, then into a showroom. Lifesize mannequin zombies and witches all start twitching and jabbering when we walk past. Angel laughs and says it works better than a burglar alarm.

Then he says, "Sorry about the mess."

"What mess?"

"Jesus, one of our warehouse staff. I swear, you can't even trust wetback labor no more."

In the back of the showroom, in an alcove dedicated to spooky lawn decorations, four more Mexicans stand around a fifth who is easy to mistake for just another prop to freak out the trick-or-treaters. He sits with his hands up like he's riding one mother of a scary rollercoaster, whimpering into the rag wadded into his mouth. The fingers on his right hand are gone from the third knuckle down, whittled to red popsicle sticks, most likely by the Craftsman belt sander resting on the bloody dropcloth next to the folding chair he's pissing in. A little guy in a big hat holds the poor bastard's arms up and whispers in his ear. Angel's silent partner, Hector Basilone.

Jesus moans over and over that he doesn't even know what he did.

"You taking him to the hospital?"

"You joking? Health care is ridiculous up here. We have universal coverage in Mexico. Not the best, but better than here. We're not doctors, but we'll take care of him, if he leans in and tells us what we asked."

He looks at me a long second. "You don't like it?"

I don't. "I'm just saying, if he's a valued employee, you might could have his accident somewhere he could still be of use to you…"

He takes me on a walk past rows of themed couples' costumes. "The hand thing, I wouldn't do it either. But it's symbolic. You understand symbols are important, right? Don't worry about us. We clean up our messes even better than we clean up yours." Angel takes me aside and offers me some chorizo and eggs. The Mexicans never stop to eat locally, and they always dress like cheap contract labor, which made them next to invisible unless a state trooper was forced to take notice. So they set up a kitchen in the breakroom and brought a cook.

"I won't trouble you with my problems, Padre. Your problems are my problems, too. So, how can I help?"

"You've been stalling on our orders, and now I see all this shit. It looks like you're moving in."

"What, this? This is just an investment in the

community. Just a little thing. We're bringing back jobs. We won't have to hide much longer, people are going to thank god we're here. It'll be the next best thing to an Indian casino, telling you. But can I confess to you? I know you're a…"

"We don't confess."

"But still, I need to get this off my chest, and now you're here, maybe we can tie up all the loose ends."

Loose ends.

"Yes, I mean… We've had a relationship for going on nine years, and that means a lot to me… but it's not like you're still buying our product like before…"

"We been over that a million times. Demand has changed, the economy is a shit sandwich…"

"It's not *my* sandwich, *padrino*. And I know you were scheming to become your own supplier. Don't lie, I got you, don't I?" The air gets heavy. "And me, big stupid Mexican that I am, I'm just going to sell you the chemicals like you're *la familia*, but now, all you *chuntara* hardasses want painkillers… Everybody wants *el goma*. Not that cheap black tar *chiva* shit from Nayarit that got all those poor white kids killed. So here we are."

"I'm just here for my order, Angel."

He bites his fingernails and spits them onto a styrofoam gargoyle. "I wish I could help you, but that's the part that hurts to confess, *jefe*. Vertical reintegration, and things of that nature. We can see where the market is growing, and it's not through you anymore. Couple hundred *gueros* here, a couple thousand there, it's crumbs, and we gotta go through a different little *jefe* in every town. We're looking to use this as a, a beachhead to hook up the whole region." Gesturing at the dusty decorations, he adds, "It's gonna be Halloween all year long."

"Was I asking for this?" I ask him.

He just shrugs. "Maybe so, maybe no."

"So I guess there's not a lot left to discuss," I say.

He nudges me back towards the stockroom. I guess Jesus still can't remember what he did wrong. He starts kicking, but he can't get away from the two guys who grab his feet and remove his shoes. Hector picks up the sander.

Angel yells in my ear as he steers me to the back door. "I do feel a little bit bad, *jefe*. But you know, regardless, if this territory was worth fighting for, someone would be fighting us for it…"

Right about now, I'm feeling every drop of venom pushing like lead buckshot through my veins to collect in my heart like another swollen black fist in the core of my chest. Sweat plasters my undershirt to my chest and streams down my face like I'm melting.

I call the clinic and get the robot operator, but I know it's open, and that's where I'm headed when I throw the truck into gear with my left hand and pull out and nearly slam into the grill of the Sheriff's truck.

Sheriff Early Ramage, Jr. jumps out and comes around before I can collect myself. He smiles at me big and pretty with a brand new set of teeth. "Getting harder every day to find something to do in this county that's still illegal, ain't it, Clyde?"

5

We're an unincorporated town that grew up around a roadhouse that sold tobacco and corn liquor and all the other things folks in Elizabeth couldn't get from the company store. No mayor or town council, but the Elizabeth sheriff got fed up running out here, so we got our own sheriff and two deputies.

Not all that walks on two legs in these parts is even half a man, but Early Ramage, Sr., was a giant, and Junior lived long and prospered in his shadow. Early Ramage, Jr., was the second of his name to wear the star, and would've retired and passed it on to his own boy, if Early III had come back from Iraq with his legs.

His boy was hard up enough for pain relief to go out of state to score harder shit than we were willing to sell. That may've been the only day of honest police work Early Ramage, Jr. actually did in his long tenure, after he ran me off the road and set my truck on fire. When the coroner's report showed his boy was full of black tar heroin, the kind young Mexican rancho kids sell out of balloons hidden in their mouths on the interstate, Junior apologized and filed a report saying my truck was totaled in an accident.

"Where's the fire, Clyde?" Early shouts, stuffing a plug of tobacco in his cheek.

With no other cards to play, I show him my hand, tell him I'm late for the clinic.

"Gotdamn, that is a caution," he leans in and takes a good, long look. Sniffs it. "The clinic? I thought you boys put your trust in the Lord. Seems like you ought to pray on it a little harder, afore God has to saw it off."

He spits a gout of brown juice down the side of my truck. "Now, I ain't one to tell another how to worship, but seems to me, if a fella get bit more n' once, maybe he ain't picking up what the Lord is trying to tell him." He laughs, waits for me to laugh, too. "Well hell, you ain't in no condition to drive, why don't you hop in mine and I'll run you over the clinic, myownself."

I beg off but he smiles real big and shakes out a cigarette, spits tobacco juice out the corner of his mouth before lights it. Shimmering rainbows of sickness revolve around Early's plastic-wrapped felt hat.

I try not to fall on him when he opens the door. I suddenly feel a lot weaker, but I manage not to claw at him as I get down and walk over to the sheriff's truck. The front passenger door is locked, but he zaps something on his keyring and the back door pops open. I look around and see no one to witness me driving off with Early.

I climb in the truck with my sick hand in my lap. Early slides behind the wheel and grins at me through the rubber-coated grate between his seat and mine, rolls up the windows and turns up the heater. "Truth to tell, when I saw you parked out behind them old stores, I feared the worst. I said to myself, 'Ol' Clyde is a rock that this whole community leans on, he wouldn't never consider doing what I think he's doing,' but it wouldn't be the first time I come across an old boy tucked out of sight with a garden hose snaked up his tailpipe, running in the window… or maybe packin' lead for lunch… but I reckon that ain't how you'd go out, right, Clyde?" He points at the hand in my lap.

The flesh around the wound is seeping through the bandages, and the discoloration is creeping out from under the hasty wrap job. It's swollen up so it looks more like a flipper.

"It was just an accident," I said. "Damn thing bit me when I was feeding it. Truth to tell, I must've got confused and forgot the old drug store was gone…"

"That sounds real good," Early said, wheeling the truck onto Main Street, passing under the banner announcing the big game tonight in Elizabeth. The local high school never goes to the championships, but the game against the Patriots is the closest we have to excitement around here, bigger than the homecoming game the week before, because nobody who don't stay ever comes home.

"And you got so confused, you wandered into that ol' Halloween store. When I saw you go in there with that bad hand, I thought you must be applyin' for a job." He chuckles and spits out the window, smoke leaking out between teeth like sugarcubes. "Yeah, my Daddy always said if you're gonna be bad, you better be fast."

I nod at that like it's real interesting, but it's all I can do not to look at the urgent care clinic as we speed right by it.

"What's the trouble, Early?"

The cruiser hums along for a bit. "Now, why would there be any trouble, Clyde? We got us a well-oiled machine up here. For once, them feds did you hillfolk some good when they clamped down on the big pharmalogical companies flooding the country with that Oxycontin and I don't know what else, y'know? Like they couldn't make enough honest dollars selling that hard-on medicine, so they come over and squeeze hard-working dealers like yourself right out the business. First they fuck the miners out of the last decent living we got in these hills, and then *that* shit? It's like seeing the last bald-eagle get all tangled in fishing line and die on a trashheap."

Early speeds up and turns onto the Palestine Road, headed south. The trapped cigarette smoke curdles into cobwebs, crawling with tiny white spiders.

"You got a point there, Early."

"Damn right. Now they'll have to go back to bushwhacking them hippie pot states, I guess. But what with that and now everybody hooked on that Oxy and fixin' to lose their Osamacare, it's a mighty big crowd gonna come lookin' for whoever can satisfy that demand... Are you pickin' up what I'm puttin' down, Reverend?"

I nod politely, looking around Early's big dumb grin. His trousers are dark green with sharp gold piping down the leg, which is good for him, because it hides stains. But his tan uniform blouse shows fresh grease stains, bright orange ones, so I can figure pretty clear I'm not being invited onto the ground floor of this once-in-a-lifetime opportunity.

"Early," I try to cut in, "we were all for giving you a flat monthly. As memory serves, it was you had to have that percentage."

He looks at me and audibly, palpably, stops smiling. "Everybody who knows you understands why you done it, Clyde. They see your cheap truck and your shitbox house, and they hear folks testify about the church doing miracles, and it was good while it lasted. But this is progress, son, and you don't stand in front of progress. This is like the mines all over again, but some of us have a chance to come out of it better off, for a change."

Early and his wife used to go to Bethesda Baptist, but like a lot of folks, they now go up to the big new church in Elizabeth, which I hear has a Starbucks and a Coldstone inside it. I hear sometimes they even get to hear about Jesus.

"That snake in my mailbox was right clever, Early. I wouldn't have figured you for the nuanced type."

"Gotdamn, Clyde! Someone put a snake in your mailbox?" He laughs hard enough to choke on his tobacco. Flips the cigarette out the window. "Hoo boy, you sure lucky you got you some police protection."

I try to tell him I need to get back to the clinic, and maybe I do, I forget. We're racing down the Palestine Road and the trees crowd up close to hide the occasional dirt driveway or trail up into the hills, and the mountaintops that've been blown off. I try not to beg for my life.

"Where we headed, Early?"

Early looks over his shoulder at me and frowns like he suddenly can't remember why we're such good friends. "Man, you should see your face. You damn sure ain't gonna throw up in my truck, I tell you that."

He fidgets a bit as he drives, lights up another cigarette and draws deep on it. "We got to go over to the rest stop on the highway to pick up a special new gal."

I close my eyes and ask for strength. I ask myself.

Early runs sporting girls along the rest stops on Route 291. The truckers pick them up and drop them off and Early ferries them around. I've paid him a monthly percentage to look away from my transgressions, but we all look away from the sheriff's own side jobs. The price of drawing breath.

"You and me go way back, so I'm asking as a friend. We gone need you to step back, and be what you always was. Just stick to the Good Book and tell your flock to keep their heads down and mouths shut, and we all gone make out alright, in the sweet by and by."

I can't think of anything else to say, so I sit and shiver and look out the window. Presently, we turn off into a sad little lot lined with semis around a restroom, a weatherbeaten shelter with worked-over snack machines and a few equally beat-up travelers and working girls lined up under the crooked awning.

Early parks. "I tell you, these young girls all want to be dominatrixes, can you beat that? You have to slap some sense into 'em. Nobody who works for a living wants to get spanked in bed. Working man gets plenty of that at work. They all run off to Richmond or Atlanta or Baltimore to put diapers on stockbrokers or some shit. I even had a girl got dudes to pay to watch her read. Just set there on her webcam."

The clouds part for a moment, just a bit of sun glinting off the dash, and Early looks down to the Coke cans in the cupholder, then back up at the rest stop again shrouded in gray.

"But far as I know, most men want to feel like a king in bed, want to knock a few teeth out, and that's their business. If he'll pay for damages, he's welcome to it. But you can't find fine young girls to be punching bags like you used to, not even the drugs'll make 'em stick around. Used to be, the MTV would show 'em what's up." Early rolls down his window, cranes his neck around, spits. "Where the fuck is that old bitch?" He bops the horn a few times and a couple girls come over, kind of herding one, who drags and sags her way out of their hands like she's gonna faint and blow away.

"This one, I had to pull her out of retirement to satisfy that demand. Lot of trucks on the road leading up to Christmas, and I'll be damned if them truckers don't actually like 'em more, the less teeth they got..."

The whores come around to the back, outside my window. Makeup like bondo over cracks and rust, shivering in tube tops and miniskirts in the cold and damp. Early points and pops the front passenger door. "Put her up front with me," he says. "Reverend back there is a happily married man. Sides, I might want to give her a taste on the way back."

The one in the middle is shuffled into the shotgun seat. She leans against the door, hunched over like her guts hurt. Early slaps her playfully. She flinches and covers her face, already sporting a freshly swollen black eye.

My heart hammers black nails into my chest. I lean up against the grate and try to stir the hair on the back of her neck with my silent cry.

Donna—

6

Early lights up another cigarette. "Yessir. Anyone who says you still can't earn a decent living out here just ain't trying. How much you make last night?" He throws an elbow into Donna's ribs.

I grab the grate and squeeze, trying to rip it down with my one good hand.

Still leaning against the window, Donna takes a damp wad of cash out of her bra and holds it out.

He takes it and pinches it open, whistles and spits. "Gotdamn! See, in one night, you made more than a month in that shitty clinic. Your talents were going to waste, girl! I tole you you'd clean up. Ain't she a looker, Clyde? She can pass for quality, but you can see in her eye, she's built to bend over. I'd let you have a taste yourself, but I know how devoted you are to your Sally. If I had me a good God-fearing woman like that, I suppose I'd be as upright and decent as you."

My heart stomps my chest like hobnail boots on broken glass. My hand swells. The bandages constrict like a boa around a mouse. "Early, you ain't got to do this…"

Early guffaws. "I ain't got to do shit, less I want to. Folks round here been gettin' some mighty queer ideas about how the world works. I don't rightly know where, maybe that Internet shit, or that radio preacher up in Elizabeth. All I know is, we all got to serve somebody…"

He undoes his zipper and reaches over to grab a hank of Donna's greasy auburn hair. She pulls back and his arm tenses, his thick, hairy thumb pivoting to go down her jaw and take hold of her throat.

"God damn you, Early Ramage. You stop this—"

"Stop? Sure, let's stop." Early smiles and pulls over within sight of the junction with Palestine Road. No car passes. Not a sound but the rumble of the idling engine and the odd plink of raindrops on the roof. "Your hand feelin' better, Reverend? Maybe you wanna get dropped home, and your Sally can meet this sweet piece of meat…"

"Just drive, Early. Please…"

Hobie Hawkins passes in his truck, slows down and exchanges a friendly wave with Early. I hunch down in his shadow until Hobie turns onto the highway and speeds off.

"Preacher, you got more problems than a Chinese algebra book, and not all the bran muffins in Branson could make anyone who matters give a shit about you. I'm the only one in town sees any use in keepin' you around, but you got to know your role. Like this sportin' gal here. You know your role, right?"

Donna turns to look at me then, one gold-flecked hazel eye piercing me with naked hate, the other closed up by purple puffy flesh. She shakes her head once, then bends down out of sight beneath Early Ramage's considerable belly.

Whistling "Coal Miner's Daughter," Early shifts the truck into Drive and puts his foot on the gas.

With the men and women of our hills for evidence, it is easy to believe that God shaped Man out of a fistful of clay in a hurry before lunch, and Woman as an afterthought from scraps. Donna's no Miss West Virginia, but anyone with eyes could tell she was shaped by gentler hands, for a softer world.

I met her when one of my retailers came back from his rounds with a ruptured nut and his eye halfway gouged out. Told me some story about how this redheaded bulldagger bitch robbed him, but I naturally saw who had the right of it.

I went looking and came across her before too long. All the other girls knew you didn't cross Donna. She told me he tried to force himself on her, so she raked his face with her keys, and would be happy to do the same for me if I wanted to try her.

She worked the truck stops around Kanahwa County without a pimp, and didn't need one. She was just playing the hand she'd been dealt, and never tried for one second to let them think she wanted it. But they kept coming, reading something in her eyes or her words or the way she wore her body that said what she was for. They always had.

She'd finished high school and got out of the hills by joining the Navy, but dropped out after getting groped by the whole chain of command. When she came back, she couldn't find work or settle down with a local boy who'd never been outside the county, and fell into drinking and eating to make herself fat so they'd leave her alone, then drugs to get skinny, and soon she found herself stripping, then giving blowjobs to truckers on the interstate.

I wasn't the first to try to save her. Maybe she turned to me because I didn't force myself on her or try to make her buy her way out. Or maybe it was because I was more doomed than she was. She had more sense than pride, and when I offered her a way out, she took it. Set her up with night school and then a job at the urgent care clinic a few years ago, but it wasn't right away that we became what we are.

Maybe if I was one man, and not two, I wouldn't have told myself I needed another. But she could see both of me as one man and never ask me why I did it. I told myself the part of me that I gave Donna was just what Sally could never accept, so I was doing her a favor. Even now, I don't know if I loved her or just loved the way she looked at me, knowing all that I was.

Right now, I just know I deserve it when she punches me in the face on Main Street.

Early lets us out in front of the clinic and drives away, still whistling. A bunch of kids and a few grizzled addicts smoke outside, waiting for the NA meeting to start. Donna bends over and vomits in the gutter. I hate myself for looking around to see who's looking before I put my hand on her back and try to lead her into the clinic.

"You got a cigarette?" she asks.

I tell her I'm sorry, but I don't. I quit ten years back, but I still keep a pack around for her and sometimes smoke with her, so I don't stick out when I smell like her.

"Where's your truck? I'll smoke one out the ashtray. You never but finish but half of them."

She rides me about that like I'm burning money. Smokes like she's underwater, breathing through a straw, smokes them down to the filter. I tell her my truck is a few blocks off, but I'll go to the Exxon and get some, and did she take her meds today?

That's when she whirls and hits me in the mouth with an uppercut. I inhale sharply and swallow a glut of blood from my lip tearing on my teeth, fall square on my ass at her feet.

Her leg goes back to kick me. "You sonofabitch," she growls. "You piece of shit, *what did you do?* He told me… this was because of you…"

I try to answer, try to apologize, but I can't. My right arm bursts into flame and a mound of bricks drops on me, crushing me into a puddle in the pavement.

All the anger drains out of her and I feel guilty for pushing the hardwired button that triggers her maternal instinct like scratching a cat makes it purr, even as I wonder why I didn't just lead with the heart attack.

The clinic is one of the better things we did with the money. Aside from a doctor and two nurses staffing a half-assed ER, they've got the only decent detox program for walking-around folks in this part of the state, with Buprenorphine, Vivitrol and methadone treatment and naloxone on-hand for overdoses. When they opened, the line went halfway to Elizabeth, because some idiot spread the word it was just another pill mill.

Naturally, she also keeps a ready stock of antivenin. When I come to, I'm lying in a bed and there's sticky EKG leads all over my chest and an IV dripping into my arm. She's sitting in a chair against the curtain. Silhouettes work over a body in the next bed, telling her to breathe, just breathe, and try to tell them what kind of drugs she had for breakfast, they're not sure if she's strong enough for them to pump her stomach. In the back room, the morning NA meeting is getting rowdy. Half the junkies in there get passes from the high school to attend.

"Was a rattler," I try to tell her, "a diamondback."

"You told me already," she says, but I don't remember it. Maybe she already knew what kind of snake it was. Nobody would blame her if I got the wrong antivenin and died right here. "We got the right dose into you on top of painkillers and the blood pressure medication you should be taking every damn day, but it was a near thing. You been bit so many times, we could use your damn blood to make antivenin…"

"What kind of painkillers?"

"Just some Percocet. Why, are you…?"

"No, no, Lord, no." I strain to lift my arm. "Bit late in the day to be taking on new addictions." The fire is snuffed out, but my hand still weighs more than my truck. "This was a bad one. The Holy Spirit wasn't with me. It caught me by surprise…"

"You had a mild heart attack, you dumb old fuck. You should've come in right away…"

"Was waiting on you."

"That's stupid. Eugene or Jenna could've fixed you up. When did you get bit, anyhow?"

"I swear, I didn't know. He—" I forget what I'm saying, where I'm going. It's nice.

"Don't matter." Her eyes get shiny. "It was bound to happen sooner or later. They don't ever let you forget what you are…"

The bustle of the clinic presses us. I speak. "That's not what you are. Everyone does what they have to, to get by." I sit up and reach out to her. "But I swear, he'll answer for it—"

"Don't. I see now, what this always was."

"That ain't true, girl, and you know it. I—"

"No, you don't. Maybe your shadow did, but you just pitied me… as low a thing as *you* are. You hurt me more than anything Early could do to me, even when we were good."

"Donna, listen. After today, it won't be safe to be here for anyone who was mixed up with me. It's all coming down. You should get out." I'm thinking how much I got stashed in the church, how much I could give her, instead of giving it to Garth.

"Don't you think I would have gone a long time ago, if I had anywhere to go? You think I was staying here for *you*? For a sick little shadow of you even your wife couldn't stomach?" She lets out a bitter laugh. "No. You did me a good turn, Clyde, but now I figure… we're even…" Choking back tears, she adjusts the flow on my IV so my arm turns to icy marble. "And don't take on after Early Ramage on my account. He at least paid me for it."

The woman in the next bed goes into cardiac arrest. The nurse working with her hollers for someone to call the ER over in Elizabeth to send the ambulance, and someone else laughs. The big kid who sweeps the floors offers to drive her up, since she's got no insurance. The woman in the bed is calling for Donna.

"God damn you, Reverend Clyde," Donna says. She gets up and pushes through a slit in the curtains before I can get out of bed.

My phone vibrates on the nightstand. I reach over for it, dreading the 1 MESSAGE icon on the screen.

It's Sally, asking when I'm coming home, and if she should make me a lunch before afternoon services.

7

I sit in the truck for a long time, wondering if I should even go in there. I look at my house now as a thing of the past, a box that holds memories that maybe never belonged to me in the first place. I think of Sally in there making food, and I hear the snake in the bag.

I take a deep breath, and go in to say goodbye.

Sally glances up from the kitchen counter. "Looks like it got to you, this time."

"Looks like it."

She pauses for a bit, looks down at her cutting board, holds the knife just over it. "You want to tell me what you did?"

"Doubted was all."

"Was it?"

"What do you want me to say?"

I see her knuckles go white. "I'd like to know the truth."

"I think you know everything you want to know."

"Is that so?"

"It is. You've played this the whole time like you didn't know. But you understand how this system works. You know the church isn't everything. If anybody knows that, it's you."

"Well, of course I do. Of course I do. I was asking," she turns around, knife still in her hand. "How you managed to fuck it up?"

The hard edge of her voice stings, so the sad knowing of it almost goes over my head. "What?"

She moves toward me. "Honey." She places her hands on my arms, knife still splayed beside my throat. "Sit down."

I sit.

"When you're out there with that snake, riling up the flock, I think that's real nice. I like the way you talk, and I like the thought of you getting bit and asking for more, like how you stare the Devil down. But I know that's not the only thing. Come on, now. When I asked you how you fucked up, I'm not asking you how you fucked up with the Lord. I'm asking you how you managed to fuck up with your *other* flock."

I let her go on.

"The reason I'm worried, baby, is that I'm afraid one of these boys might get the wrong idea about Sally Hilburn. I'm worried that they might get it in their mind that since Clyde fucked up, maybe the way to show him a thing or two is to roll by his house, and set a couple of waterheads on Sally. Get her good. You know, to show him."

My stomach drops.

"And then, maybe if that's not enough, maybe if you really fucked up, maybe we'll roll through and finish her off. Poor thing'll be all used up anyway. So why not? Put a bullet in her. Or torture her and film it and send it to Clyde. Because it's all about this sad-sack redneck fuckup, and how *he* feels about this shit. Well, buddy I'll tell you something. Last man dumb enough to touch me without me saying so, do you remember Jeffrey Gray?"

I remember. Football player, nice guy. Strong, silent type. Scholarship got him out to play college ball, got him everywhere but here.

"Yeah, back in school I had a thing for Jeff, but I didn't have a thing for being touched. He tried, and you know what I did?"

"No."

"I bit his tongue off."

Explains the "silent" part.

"I'm not worried about me, is what I'm trying to tell you, Clyde. I'm worried about *you*. And I want to know if there's anything I can do to help you out of the shit you've sunk into."

I shake my head.

Sally sighs. All of a sudden, she's a stranger to me. "It's been a lot of fun, Clyde. I appreciate everything you've done for this family. I appreciate everything you've done for me. I love you, baby."

I can't bring myself to answer.

"But you need to get the fuck out, and fix what you've done."

I get up and storm for the door.

I try not to hear what she says as I push the screen door open, but it leaps and grabs onto the bottom of my ear and crawls its way into my brain:

"Whatever that might entail."

8

My Daddy was seventeen when his Daddy went missing.

His two sisters, Rebecca and Zealia, were nineteen and fourteen, and his little brother Huey was only nine. The church was bigger back then, but still poor, as anyone who earned a good living wanted to hear Jesus cheer on their good fortune, while Granddaddy's gospel was the hard truth for those with nothing to lose and no chance to win. And nobody needed that gospel more than the Hilburn clan.

Great-Granddaddy Hilburn, according to legend, had his second awakening when he hid in a holiness church in Kentucky while running from the law after he stole a car and robbed a string of gas stations. Grateful for his deliverance, he came home and opened the church in Two Run Hollow. His son took to the pulpit early on, and carried on when Great-Granddaddy died of a snakebite.

The church limped on, with membership dropping down to the hundred-odd folks it still is today, after so many went west with the second world war, and so did the family. Grandma was sickly after Huey was born, and lay abed most days and nights in a room of her own.

Daddy wasn't so keen on following the family calling. He fancied himself something of a singer, so the stories went, and though his father and the church condemned secular music as an abomination that led to miscegenation and damnation, he held girls spellbound with his voice and his hare-brained schemes of lighting out for Nashville to get discovered. He was courting the one who would become my mother when Zealia tried to hang herself from a cedar behind the outhouse. Daddy found her and cut her down, and when she got her breath, she told him the truth about their family.

Maybe my grandmother refused Granddaddy one too many times, or maybe he just couldn't help himself. Maybe he was so secure in his righteousness, that he knew the Lord wanted him to bed Rebecca, and give her a child. Mama was only told Rebecca got herself pregnant and wouldn't name the father, but she had to *know*, though she agreed to claim Huey as her own if they'd only let her sleep.

Zealia said lately, Granddaddy had started to take notice of her. Mama hated her like poison. Rebecca warned her but couldn't bring herself to stand up for her little sister. With my daddy going to Nashville, there'd be no one to stop it all happening again.

Everyone had their own ideas about what happened to Granddaddy. Some said he lit out on his family to start over somewhere else that rainy night, that he'd always had the devil in him like all them Hilburns, and it finally won out. Some said he was murdered by his own son for standing in the way of his foolish dreams of stardom. Some of the wilder, meaner speculations even came close to the truth.

Daddy ran off only a week or two later, and the church had to make do with a couple deacons who couldn't read their own names, let alone the Bible. Grandma burned her house down around her drunk and smoking shortly after Rebecca married the mailman and moved down to Richmond. Zealia took up with Hobie Hawkins, eventually giving him four fine sons.

The state police looked for Daddy, but he didn't go to Tennessee like he told everyone. He enlisted in the Marines using a doctored birth certificate and served a two-year hitch in Vietnam. Came back in '68 with a hook for a hand and half his face burnt off and a bitter look in his good eye like he'd been cheated out of worse, to find a son waiting for him.

Huey lived with us, but as soon as he was able, he set up in a shotgun shack up at the end of the trail on Gum Run. He lives there still, and does as much for the church as he can without speaking. He ain't mute, he just don't talk. But he sings like a redneck angel, and builds things out of glue and pennies. His model of the London Bridge is six feet long, and got him wrote up in *Ripley's Believe It Or Not!*

Twenty years ago, just after Daddy died, the local coal refinery choked Two Run Creek with a hundred tons of slurry. During the cleanup, they found a headless skeleton in a ruined raincoat with a shotgun tied to his hand with fishing line.

They figured he must've sat on a rock above the creek that night and blown his brains out so he'd fall dead in the rushing water and perhaps go missing forever, ending his sordid biography in a question mark. The rocks in the ruined raincoat bore out a verdict of suicide, and the remains of a leatherette bible in his pocket identified him as the Reverend Glory Hilburn.

The harmonica that was also in his pocket under all the rocks was impossible to fingerprint or trace, and the fact that the nylon that tied the shotgun to his no-doubt trembling hand in the fateful final moment, was actually taken from a cheap acoustic guitar, never stirred even the meanest gossips to speculate about what really happened to Glory Hilburn in mixed company.

9

Before the elbow bend on 89, there's a changeable roadboard like you'd see out in front of a diner that says "Holiness Pentacostal Church of God With Signs Following," held down by cinderblocks. No special verse, nothing clever, just the name is all.

I turn right in front of the sign and stop instinctually at the mailbox. I think better of it and drive up the approachment through the pin oak branches to where the church sits in a slight clearing. All of four trucks, two minivans, and a couple bikes parked off down the hill, from what I can see. Without the sun on it the building appears featureless, same as the recently added children's buildings behind it. Three squat buildings with corrugated tin roofs connected by crisscrossing wood ramps. My kingdom.

Feels like I'm up high in the trees, nothing else around, like I might fall and it'd be alright if I did.

I take a minute to think on what I might say. I get out the truck. For a moment it seems impossibly quiet, then I hear the cicadas, and then them underneath.

They are in the vestibule, washing each other's feet, when I come in. The women wash the men and the men wash the women, eyes averted, intent on the ritual. The faint green mold and dust odor, the muted splashing and murmured prayers, slow my heartbeat like a drug.

Lee Sweet and Clem Lathrop brace me at the door. Clem blesses me and they pray for a long minute with their hands on my shoulders. "You ought not to be walking round like that," Lee says. Clem has a sermon prepared, but he looks tired, and gratefully folds when I tell him I need to say a few words.

I take one of the high old wooden chairs and June Snodgrass and Elvie Gunn unlace my cracked black shoes and roll off my socks rancid with sweat. As they lave my feet in cold wellspring water in the galvanized tin tub, they say, "Lift him up, Lord," over and over, and I remember the shameful moments in my youth when this simple ritual gave me a sore erection.

The congregation sings the regular hymns, then Huey comes up and sings "Were You There When They Crucified My Lord" as soft as morning dew on rose petals. He once made a cross, ten foot high, with a life-sized Jesus nailed to it, out of glued-together pennies. Ripley's folks came to see him about buying it for their

Odditorium in Branson, but he turned them down cold. I've heard children say at Sunday school he's a sineater—that he takes his meals off the chests of the recently deceased at their wakes, that he eats up their worldly faults so they can go to glory.

At churches like ours, the parking lot outside is no measure of who's inside. When I take my place at the table, the room is still filling up. Folks who only come Sundays heard about my hand, and word got around. They can't help but stare. Huey stands in the back like he always does, the sleepy look on the unlovely monument of his face telling you he was invisible to everyone else, only you could see him.

"This morning," I start, "as you may've heard, I got bit." Gripping the corners of the table where my daddy and great-granddaddy each dropped dead on their last day preaching, where my daddy first preached the day after he killed my granddaddy, "Now, some who don't know us might think we take up snakes thinking we won't ever get bit…"

Heads shake vehemently all through the room.

"Nothing in this life ever told us to expect anything more than our share of venom. We shun this world and dare him to take us away from it, so fiercely do we believe.

"But I wish I could believe, oh you simple sinners… I wish to fucking God I could believe that God did not exist."

The room grumbles, wide white eyes and round, black mouths.

"It would be so goddamn easy to be a preacher, if God didn't exist. He could be whatever you want Him to be… father, mother, best friend, a faithful lapdog… So easy to spread the word of His infinite love and the glory of His light, if He was not real. I could offer words of comfort, tidings of joy.

"I would dearly love to tell you poor dumb fuckers that lie. But His love is the love of a greedy man for money, of a spoiled boy for the candles on his birthday cake, and His light is the reflection off His terrible face of our burning in a fire called time."

I mop sweat from my brow. It smells sour.

"No shit. It would be so easy to tell you that He will reward your obedience and punish you for your sins, that He is always watching, and so you must be good. But we know we are none of us pure enough to enter the Kingdom of Heaven, for we are just as He made us, and it is only our faith, not our evil, that leaves us lower than the least of those cried for on the TV.

"No one is closer to God than us, I say, and it's true, because God doesn't make mistakes, so He surely must love fools. Fools who weep that they cannot still sell the last black bones of these hills, and strip bare the last few patches of healthy land they have left. Who else would throw their souls away so cheaply as we have, to have twisted our miserable poverty into a mantle of terrible pride? To cling to our dead faith like a goddamn wet electric blanket?"

They look to each other, they look back, they look at the ceiling. The building settles.

"You know me, and I thank you for turning a blind eye all these years for whatever good my evil did, but you know I was always the worst among you. The threat of divine punishment seldom stops a man or woman from giving into the evil in their hearts. We tell ourselves that our faith keeps us from becoming animals like those who don't believe. Folks who don't believe in God don't need the whip to control their lives. Nobody needs the Lord more or prays harder than you and I, who've got nothing else. Maybe we're the ones who hate Him, because we know He's there, and the pipedream of escaping His wrath is all that stops us from being devils, and yet we know we mean not a goddamn thing to Him."

With my good hand, I take up the snake. It's a big old cottonmouth, nearly four foot long, and I lift it up with some difficulty. "The truth is that we do this not to demonstrate how God knows us for His favored elect, but to dare Him to deliver us from this fire, because the promise of Hell looks like a sweet summer Sunday after this cruel and useless school, where every trouble and tragedy is a test we're doomed to fail, and all that is beautiful, all that gives ease or comfort or pleasure, is a snare of the devil.

"In Jesus' name, we pray…" Using both hands now, I hold the snake high over my head and I try to let the original tongue come. The bad blood in my bit hand sloshes and spills down out of my wound and floods my heart like wet cement. Sweat burns and blinds me. I speak the well-worn nonsense noises that trigger that involuntary song of our savage faith, that numb my brain so my spirit can fly.

"Kaanamakaalajeramaaa…"

My throat tears with its howling and my hand trembles and the snake twists and coils with anxiety and I squeeze and shake it and scream into its face to take me.

The room is uncannily quiet, the others frozen, watching, untouched by the spirit that I beg to take me, but their mouths work, their hands clutch, and I know my words did their work. In any service, the crowd gets lifted up by the freedom of delirium. Words and sense fall away, and they're free to wordlessly curse God and all of creation, all of their lives and themselves, to dare Him to take us away. Some nights, what we give up is like a long, collective spiritual orgasm. Other nights, we sound like livestock who just realized what goes on in a slaughterhouse.

Right now, they're rooting for the snake to bite me

almost as hard as I am. The tangle of snakes in the cage hiss and bite each other in ferocious knots. Lee Sweet balks but Clem reaches in and takes one and it immediately bites him on his wrist, but no one moves to help him.

"Kaanamakaalajeramaaa…"
letmeoutletmeupletmebedead

Holding the snake up to my face, I pinch its jaws open like a purse. My hand shakes like a junkie with the needle. *I have sinned against you*, I scream at the snake in my wordless words. *Strike me down, if you dare—Take me—please—*

There is a click like a lock turning, and the cottonmouth dies, the beautiful undulating muscle a tube of cold meat in my hands, its venom no match for mine.

I lower it to the plain table that has always been our pulpit. I back away from it, eyes downcast but skin prickling with the eyes of my flock, unwilling witnesses to an unacceptable miracle.

No one stops me as I stumble out of the church without my shoes. I weave through the junkyard of parked cars to my truck off by itself at the far corner, where the dirt lot succumbs to chicory and hollyhocks and blackberry.

I fumble with my keys. I tear open the door and grab up the canvas bag. It thrashes with sullen fury. I undo the knot with my teeth and plunge my bad hand in and before I can lift it out, the rattler's fangs plunge home through the bandages and it's weaker, this time, but the white fire runs up my arms and I sag across the seat, *Thank you, Lord—thank you—*

Behold, I give unto you power to tread on serpents and scorpions, and over all the power of the enemy: and nothing shall by any means hurt you.

—Luke 10:19

10

I lie beneath a low, spreading fruit tree in full bloom, in a clearing in an overgrown garden. The full moon is an overripe magnolia blossom dripping molten gold on the trees and the eyes of the animals watching from the shadows.

The Snake dangles from a low branch to hold me fixed by its mesmeric golden gaze. She is black and beautiful and he is silver and terrible, both of them are the Snake.

"You are with me now," says the Snake, "and there are no more lies here."

"Ain't you gonna offer me an apple?"

The Snake smiles. It isn't a human smile on a human face, but somehow it comes across. "That's not what you're asking for. Why do you hate me, who only ever gave you the truth?"

I itch all over with uncontrollable lust. "You were the author of man's fall."

"You were destined to fall, as I was destined to tempt you."

I cross my arms to trap my burning hands. Blisters erupt wherever my skin touched the snake. "Man may not have a choice but to give in to sin, but he can repent."

"I could never repent, because that was not my role, any more than it's yours. Heaven needs Hell. And Man needs a scapegoat for all the lies he tells himself."

The blisters burst on my palms. Buds emerge and open dewy petals—roses, orchids, lilies, honeysuckle and magnolia. Their perfume makes me drunk. "I don't need *you* to tell me about lies."

"Lies are all that separate you from the animals, O Man. And your biggest lie? God is your way of telling yourself you can never change, that you are still good when you are doing bad, because no matter how miserable your life is, an invisible absent father loves you, so long as you never admit the truth."

My blood rushes and I cannot resist touching myself between my legs. My flowery hands caress my erection and cut themselves on scales. I realize where the snake comes from. "What truth is that?"

"That there was always another way. That it's never too late to change, if you'll only accept the world for what it is. That you could create beauty and change the world, if you could only accept yourself. That the fear of Hell is not half so frightening to you, as the reality that you always had a choice, that you are only a child of yourself."

The flowers run riot up my arms and chest, feeding on me. I rip them out and crush them in my hands and the fragrance is like the smell of newborn babies. Their roots tear out clods of my crumbling gray flesh. "I know I'm a piece of shit. I've sinned, and I aim to pay for it."

The Snake entwines around me, squeezes out my breath. "No one gets what they paid for, O Man. You get what you make. You've taken much. And how do you aim to pay for it? If all of this is God's plan, then you were born to belong to me. And if all of this is one of God's little mistakes, then what fucking good is God?"

Not in love or drugs or even prayer have I known such pleasure as I feel when the Snake crushes me like a flower.

11

My phone is buzzing when I wake up in the truck.

It's from Lorna Gunn. I stare at the message many times before I can read the words.

U want WAR??? Walmart RIGHT NOW or UR HOUSE in 1 hr!!!

The bag is empty, trapped in my paralyzed, blackened hand. I drop it on the floor and notice the phony parcel that was jammed in my mailbox with the snake, lying there under the briefcase, and in my fury I cannot recall if I brought it with me or if it is another shitty miracle.

I reach for it, but then I hear the snake stir under the seat, coiled among the springs. I hear it speak. I hear it tell me I've been denied again because I have to suffer this. I have to make this right, before I can know the relief of burning forever.

Someone knocks on my window and I shake myself.

My shorts cling to my crotch in a shameful mess. I tell them to go away.

It's Lee. Says something about how Clem refused medical treatment and went home to pray, and asks if I need anything.

I hastily pop the briefcase and drop the parcel in it, snap it shut and shove it under the seat. I tell him I need to get to the Walmart in Elizabeth. And my shoes.

He sheepishly holds them up and says to slide over, he'll drive me. I think of what's under the seat, and I tell him we're taking his Mercury.

Clem and Lee have always been my right hand in the church and my left in the dark. They followed down the path I led them like it was any other duty as a deacon of the church. The closest I had to a friend in school and after, Clem was as true and loyal as any dog, and smarter than about half of them. I often suspected that Lee was willing to go along simply due to his nature. A confirmed bachelor who lived alone in an apartment above a vacant storefront on Main, he ate with us most holidays and called the church his only family.

They helped me when the Dixie Mafia tried to sell drugs in our valley. We had to break arms and burn trailers at first to demonstrate that we were just blood simple enough to do any damned thing, but when they came to kill me, I prayed with the man they sent and struck a bargain that tied us to the Gunn clan, the local Dixie franchise. We bought marijuana from hill people who'd seen the burley tobacco market dwindle away, and sold it to low-country folks who could afford it. We sold speed to truckers and other folks working two jobs just to stay on the bright side of piss-poor. We would control the sale of any illegal drugs, and no outside crew would ever operate in our mountains.

When the pill mills came to Appalachia, the mines were long gone, and too many local folks who weren't hooked on oxycodone saw crooked doctors for pills to sell to the unlucky ones who were. Everyone went broke and took to stealing, and many who got rich got robbed or worse before they could move away. Pills became currency. Some folks never even saw cash money. Even without gang warfare, bodies started to pile up as folks overdosed on Oxys or on that cheap black tar heroin up from Mexico. Dozens in every town; high school football stars and cheerleaders, the quality people's kids. The government finally caught up with the drug company, but they had too many lawyers for any talk of jail time, and paid a handsome settlement amounting to about a month's profits.

Almost none of that happened in Palestine. We ran two shady doctors who pushed OxyContin out of town, and kept heroin out altogether until folks like Early Ramage III started going upstate to score. When we had to, we sold low-dose generic oxycodone and stepped-on brown Mexican heroin. We got some to detox or switch to methadone before they dropped dead or broke into each other's trailers to feed their habit. I knew people would always spend what little they had to ease their pain, and I did what I could to keep them alive and keep their money here.

We will be judged for how we treated the least of these, but *we* were the least, and nobody raised a hand to help us. A lot of folks have lights and running water and toys at Christmas for children who didn't die in the womb because we did what we did.

I'm not making excuses. I saw bad folks feeding on weak ones, and good ones going hungry. I drove out the bad and protected the weak from themselves, and let them feed the good. For a while it worked, and You never said a word.

Until today, nobody who didn't deserve it got hurt. Bad folks never came around, and even the rich folks who might otherwise walk on us, the timber, mining and bank people, they knew if they treated us like poor white trash, there'd be a hand on their shoulder in the dark.

They knew angels watched over our mountains, but we were devils in our wrath.

Cody Goodfellow & J David Osborne

* * *

We pull into the Walmart parking lot in Lee's Mercury on the far side of Elizabeth just after the sun goes down. Mostly empty because of the game, but a good chunk of it, nearly a third, is taken up by trailers and motor homes and campers—what Sally likes to call the Walmartians. Folks on highway vacations tend to pile up here in autumn as retirees and vacationers and more than a few white trash gypsy Travelers who wandered off the interstate try to find their way out of our little corner of creation. Folks are walking dogs, grilling bratwurst and playing cards in the great outdoors of their parking spaces.

The Gunns' big candy-apple red lifted pickup towers over its neighbors in the last row of cars before the trailer park. We pull into the lone handicapped spot at the front, just across from the big doors, and wait.

Lee runs his mouth about all the good we done, about how half the town would still be drinking fracking wastewater from a well by candlelight, how Clem's daughter-in-law might've died giving birth to his only granddaughter if we didn't do what we done, and nobody got hurt for so long, why it should change is beyond him. He says more I don't hear because I'm thinking about that snake and wondering how I can make it kill me. I'm thinking how since my sin was pride, maybe just tearing down all the bad I done will be just like one rat tearing the other's guts out as the ship sinks. Maybe to atone for my pride, I have to raze everything *good* I thought I did, and let the bad stand as my rightful testament.

When I roll down the window, the chill wind carries the thundering drums and howling horns of the Palestine Ramblers' battle anthem from the football field up the road a bit. You can hear the local crowd booing like cows gone to slaughter, unsure for a fleeting instant if they'll end the night wearing our asses for a hat like they do every year. The drums rise defiantly above them, an angry monster's racing pulse that runs my blood up so I can look away from the swelling black hand trapped between my knees and ask Lee if he's got a gun.

"It's under my seat, like always," he says, reaching for it, "but I ain't had to so much as point it at nobody in a dog's age, and I don't even carry no bullets with it…"

I tell him to forget it.

"You gone go over there?"

No, I tell him, I'm going to wait for them to come to us. Keep it as public as possible, because if anyone in my social circle would put a snake in my mailbox, it'd be the Gunns.

"You yellow, dog-dick cocksucker," Lorna says. She

comes strutting up and flicks her cigarette butt in my open window. Lee picks it up off the floorboard, blesses it and stubs it out.

I get out the car, trying to make myself study her eyes as she looks at my hand. Her greenish-black hair is up in pigtails, her face made up for war. All the piss seems to leak out of her for just a moment. Staring solemnly like a devout pilgrim, she says in a voice of steel wool, "You got bit?"

I nod and show her. The dead flesh around the first wound almost glows under the rust-colored lamplight. The second one is a blister the size of an eye full of bad blood, with spokes of corruption radiating out from it halfway around my wrist. "I done prayed on this," I tell her.

Two of her cousins come up. One nods and smiles at me like he probably does right before he flushes the toilet every morning, but the other one, the big one, keeps one ear cocked for the sound of the football game. The big boy used to play, I remember. Used to be good.

Arkie and Bama were so named not because they were from those states, but because they were the furthest away, respectively, the local boys had ever been from home. Lorna had never been out of the county, but only a fool would count her less canny than the boys for all that, or less vicious.

They break tradition in other ways, too. Arkie, the little one, is also the dumber, uglier one, what with a cleft palate and a lazy eye, but that hardly makes Bama a spelling bee champ. Given that the window between too dumb to live and too smart for your own good up where the Gunns live and breed is narrower than a Baptist's sexual menu, they excel at a certain kind of cunning, a ferocious husbandry of grudges and a lot of places to hide their mistakes. Like our army the last couple wars, they kill more folks on accident than on purpose.

"Serves you right," she says, "if you're doing what people say you done."

"It's been a real trying day, Lorna, and I still ain't had a proper breakfast. I don't know half of what I done, let alone what folks're saying, so you'll have to catch me up."

The Gunns peddled our crank, grass and heroin. Once the market began to turn, we doubled down and had them cooking for us, too. For pills, we turned to Lorna's cousin, Ray Dean, a pharmacist at the Rexall who oversaw the prescription scheme whereby he got caught red-handed with three million Oxycontin pills prescribed for a couple dozen folks in Kanahwa County. The feds took him and a doctor in Elizabeth, and two more lost their licenses. The corporation that sold the pills got a fine and a sternly worded letter.

Ray Dean Gunn held his mud and convinced the feds he was just a go-getter who came up with the idea listening to the Rush Limbaugh show, and because a big corporation with tame senators on each hip was waist-deep in it, they just wanted it to go away. I hear the politicians say these businesses are people now, which I guess is progress, though it makes the rest of us too small to see with the naked corporate eye. When corporations die, do they go to Heaven? Are their souls bigger, brighter than ours? Are you so dazzled by them that you can't see us anymore?

Lorna was plenty sure her other cousins could switch their labs from meth to painkillers, and I trusted her enough to borrow from Garth to back her. And I won't lie, if it hadn't all blown up in my face this morning, I don't suppose I'd be regretting any of it. I doubt like Hell I'd be telling any of this to you…

She lights a cigarette, and blows menthol smoke in my face. "You tossed us to the law, little man. You think we just dumb moonshiners you can throw away, to do a deal with the motherfuckin' cartels?"

"I don't understand half of what you're saying… but I got to tell you—"

"Everybody said you were gonna sell us out soon as it suited you. Now there's goddamn beaners setting up shop on Main Street, Clyde. Tell me I'm lying."

"I didn't know nothing about that until today, myself."

"Bullshit! And you didn't sic the sheriff on us last night, either…"

I recall Early's hungover look from this morning. "What did Early do?"

"Goddamn deputies raided the lab, Clyde. The big one. But they didn't arrest nobody. Just locked it up tight with Skeet and Big Sean inside, and they burned it down."

Will this day of surprises never end?

"I'm sorry, Lorna. You sure it was Early's boys?"

"He wasn't there, but don't I know every lawman in this cocksucking county? And they sure as fuck know to leave us alone. We pay off Biloxi, you pay off the local law, that was always the deal. But there was a goddamn Mexican in the back of one of their squad cars. Little shitbird in a big black hat. Deputies talked to him in Spanish. Took his order just like at fuckin' Taco Bell."

"Ain't no Mexicans work at Taco Bell," Arkie says, "or I damn straight wouldn't eat there."

She zaps him with a stare that leaves him a few inches shorter.

"I am sorry for your loss, Lorna. I truly am. I didn't have nothin' to do with it. I didn't change sides. But as of today… It's over. We are out of the whole game. You Gunns can do what you want anywhere but Palestine, but whoever comes after me won't stand for it." I start to get back in the car.

"Clyde, you come back here. This shit ain't over. We got blood money coming to us, but we'll settle for blood."

I lean on the car roof. "There's nothing to say, Lorna. We've no more blood to spare." I sit down in the seat like it was a fifty-foot fall.

Lee turns the key in the ignition.

Bama taps the window with a twelve-gauge cut down short as a pistol. "Why don't you just gimme them keys, faggot," he says.

Lee turns to look at me and asks what he ought to do while his hand creeps down between his legs to reach under the seat for that empty gun, when Bama blows his face all over me.

12

My ears ringing. Glass teeth in my skin. His blood and mine the only color I can see. I start to get out and all I know is I'm going to face Lorna and make her settle it.

She points a pistol at me. The windshield caves in and she jumps and spins in mid-air, as a split-second later the flat wooden clap of an assault rifle finally drowns out the damn football game.

Over the dashboard, I spy a chunky bald man in a hooded Tarheels sweatshirt with an AR-15 braced, blasting from the hip like John goddamn Wayne at Iwo Jima.

Bama drops out of sight. Arkie goes sprinting for his truck. Lorna ducks behind Lee's engine block and fires at the trailer. Tarheel hunkers down behind his gas grill just as some other retired-looking tailgater comes out of an Itasca motorhome with Texas plates and fires a 9mm automatic at us. But the moment he starts to really enjoy this sudden gunowner's holiday, the Tarheel pops up in reflexive defense and opens up on Texas.

No one is trying to shoot me. I get out of the car. In this moment, I don't want to die. I just want to live long enough to go to Walmart.

People watching from just inside the doors make me turn around when Arkie comes running back up a row of cars, wildly spraying the trailer park with some kind of assault rifle he probably stole from the future. One of his stray bullets finally does the obvious, and hits the Tarheel's propane tank.

A big fireball licks up higher than the streetlamps and you can hear the Ramblers' rally cry fall silent at the game in the second between the dull thunderclap of the explosion and the echo off the face of the mountains.

I pass Del the greeter, a Nam vet with all his medals, citations and campaign fruit salad on his blue vest, rearing back in his wheelchair clutching his chest, his face the color of bad bologna. Shoulder through the crowd, spitting bits of Lee's brains on the floor, bury myself in them as they back away, thankful no one recognizes me under all this blood—

The windows shatter as Arkie shoots them out like he just heard the trumpets of Armageddon, and all accounts must be settled before the clock runs out. He yells something, but I can barely hear the shots fired for the bright white tone in my head.

The mob of shoppers comes running from the doors like hens in a foxhouse, going to ground in the checkout stands and the seasonal Thanksgiving and Christmas displays and screaming into their phones.

Overhead I hear Weather Channel muzak, bright halogen lights turning the blood in my hands neon, or maybe it's the poison. The tiles crawl over each other like a pile of box turtles swirling pink and purple and the shelves are a hundred feet high and stocked with bags of communion wafers and bottles of wine.

I think I'm running but not fast enough. Bama calls out, "Preacher!" and shoots at me from close to thirty yards away as he comes running. I feel pellets sting and the dairycase caves in behind me.

I grab blindly at shelves as I round a corner to put the fridge between me and the shooting. I've got a fourteen-ounce can of pumpkin filling in my left hand. I wrack my brains trying to remember which direction is sporting goods.

A piercing digital siren wails from the back of the store. Employees shove shoppers towards the fire exit. Customers crawl under display racks. I can hear Arkie yodeling and shooting on the far side of the store. Hosing down the wall of TV sets. Guy Fieri still grinning on one of them, split off into pixelated green and blue, sputtering in and out, shoving dripping barbecue into his mouth. I run in the other direction, turn a corner to find Bama with his back to me, hollering for Lorna. My arm snaps up. I throw the can at his head. He spins and blasts at me with the hogleg. The can explodes in the air between us, an orange sunburst of shrapnel. I skid and grab a shelf to pivot and run back the way I came. He empties the other barrel into an endcap display of deluxe deep fryers. Pain like hot grease shoots down the back of my arm.

I grab anything passing by and come back around the other side.

Bama's right where I left him. Hogleg broken open and a shell clenched in his teeth. I set after him. "Well, shit," he says, and grabs for a pistol in his waistband.

I swing this new-fangled Calphalon no-stick surface skillet backhanded. It hits him in the cheekbone. He spits shells and teeth and stumbles backwards. I can't vouch for the no-stick surface, because all kinds of Bama are stuck to it, but it makes a nice bell-like tone when I bring it back around to the other side of his face.Bama staggers backwards. I go for his pistol. I almost touch it.

Arkie skids past the aisle, boots sliding on the waxy floor. He doubles back and shoots over my head. I fling the skillet and run. My back is burning. He's shooting. It's impossibly loud. I dive and crawl and grab and throw but I'm only in camping gear, tents and sleeping bags and stoves and shit you can't seriously hurt anybody with. Smell of new nylon and cordite lingering in the air like a sound.

Bullets punch through the walls of the tents and chew a cardboard cut-out of the Duck Dynasty boys all to shit and bits of orange vest are flying in front and behind me and Arkie's bellowing, "Get up, little brother!"

Through the toy section, I pass three junkies packing an empty box for a Little Tykes plastic slide with game consoles, Blu-Ray players and Beats by Dre headphones and stuffing DVD's down their saggy jeans, and I note with dismay that two of them are Hobie Hawkins' boys.

I hop over shoppers facedown playing dead and at last, I come to the sporting goods counter. I jump on the glass to go over the counter, eyes on the rack of rifles. A kid with volcanic acne points a shotgun at me, says, "Stay back, or I'll shoot."

"Son," I say, sweet as diabetes, "I'd like to buy a shotgun."

He blinks, looks around. "It's an emergency. You have to leave."

"It sure is, son. Why I need a gun. You hear that?"

A salvo of shots. Fluorescent light fixtures explode and half of sporting goods is plunged into sparks and shadows.

"I can't just…"

"Son, don't you know the customer is always right?" I don't know where this calm is coming from. For only a minute, I'm just a customer. I point over his shoulder. "That one there, the twelve-gauge. And a box of shells, if you please. And I'd appreciate a little hustle." I slap a wad of twenties on the counter.

He just winces at me. "I don't have the keys to the counter… Jimmy… he went on break…"

"Fine," I say, and I take the one in his hands. He squeezes the trigger as it leaves his hands, reminding me to flip off the safety. I rack the pump and it's not even loaded.

Arkie pops up from behind a wall of footballs, shoulders the rifle and fires and wouldn't you know it, his futuristic machinegun gets a good old-fashioned jam. "Piece of shit—"

I grab the shells off the counter, pinning the gun barrel-down between my knees. Tear open the carton with my teeth and pinch out a shell, shove it awkward as hell into the breech, then another, look up at Arkie snapping a fresh magazine into his rifle.

Another shell, then another.

Arkie points the rifle at me. "Flat on the floor, goddamnit!" He yells at the clerk: "Hey boy, you know anything about Steyr rifles?"

I brace the shotgun on my knee, steady it good as I can with my right and grip the trigger backwards with my left and I blast fifty footballs. Arkie skitters out of sight, giggling like Woody Woodpecker.

I come after him, adrenaline turning to lead in my blood. I need to run him down before he can get his fancy eurotrash rifle fixed. Need to kill him before he can kill me.

"C'mon then, bad boy!" He's screaming and giggling so I can see him before I see him. Come around the corner and right there I jerk the trigger. Barrel flies up off my right arm when I shoot the chubby young man he's holding like a shield right in his unmanly bosoms. The kid clawing at his exposed ribs, coughing blood.

"Nice shootin', chief!" Arkie cackles. Shoves the dead kid at me and climbs up the shelves and vaults over the top into the next aisle.

I'm staring at this dead young man in baggy pants made out of an American flag and my mind ponders how wearing Old Glory like a diaper is less disrespectful than burning it. I guess my brain can be quick to grab what it can, to make me feel better about a bad mistake, and that's all this is. All this whole goddamn day is: a Bible-sized string of stupid mistakes.

I turn the shotgun to put the stock on my knee and pump out the spent shell with my left hand, looking at the floor, at Arkie's dropped rifle and a whole mess of Blu-Rays and Xbox games, Flamin' Jalapeno Cheetos and Rockstar energy drinks this guy must've picked out before we came in the store. Had one hell of a weekend planned.

I must still be looking at all this shit when Arkie comes back.

Vaulting over the top shelf like a white trash samurai with an aluminum baseball bat in each hand. Comes down swinging on my head as I duck and connects with my right shoulder.

My arm goes numb. God bless numbness. His other bat hits me in the left side of my head, right on my fuckin ear and somehow finds a nerve that hasn't already screamed itself hoarse today.

I'm falling and he's falling on me, knees up to cave in my chest, riding me to the floor. I lose my grip on the gun. It falls between us. My ass hits, then the gun butt hits and goes off between us. Everything south of Arkie's nose flies up and comes back to rain down on my face.

Blind, all I can see is red…

My face burns and bleeds from a hundred holes, but I mop the meat out of my eyes and Arkie crawls backwards slowly like half a rat out of a trap. His eyes fixed on me with a terrible instant wisdom, tongue flapping out of the hollow where his jaw used to be.

All I hear is sirens. I run for the front. Come down the power aisle to see Lorna holding her own against the combined might of the trailer park from behind an improvised barricade of shopping carts. Bama comes out of the next aisle. Sees me and waves. She turns to shoot at me my hands up I just don't can't—

They light her up from behind, five then ten red mouths opening up to say grace. As she falls, Bama runs out to catch her and he finally goes down too.

I see red and blue lights flashing out front and I turn and shag it back to the fire exit and there's a paramedic and a deputy with his hands full running triage on a mob of sobbing shoppers and when someone takes my arm and leads me aside, I'm just grateful but I can't hear what he's saying for the ringing in my ears and I can't see too good through the swelling and the gore on my face, so I'm all the way in the back of his car before I realize I'm not in an ambulance.

Garth shouts in my ear real loud so I can hear him. "You ready to go to church, old man?"

13

Once when I was seven, I rode with my Daddy in his truck down to my mother's people in Burning Springs, when, just a mile out of town, we hit a deer.

Daddy told me to stay in the truck and he climbed down and went over to where it lay in a ditch. I tried to stay put like he said, but he knelt over it for a long time with his head bowed down, and its head on his knee. I got out but didn't come close. I remember its legs kicking feebly and giving little jerks as the broken bones tore it up inside. He turned and saw me and ordered me back to the truck, and I got in and waited for him.

Next day, when my mother's brother took me back, I led some kids from school—mostly uppity kids from the Baptist church who called us heathen freaks, but I recall that even then, Lee was there—down the road to see it. And how I beamed when they saw the skid marks and the spot of blood and the matted red grass in the ditch, but the carcass was gone.

Someone told someone who told my Daddy, who beat me bloody when I came home for taking the kids out of town, for going to see what he forbade me to look upon. I cried with pain, but I was fiercely proud of him until dinner.

I cried as I ate the tough, gamy venison steak, and he almost beat me again for being weak. I couldn't tell him I was crying because I had really believed that he had healed the deer, and sent it back into the forest.

Big cities have these famous rivalries. Yankees or the Mets. Lakers or the Clippers. Here we had Walmart or K-mart. And K-Mart lost that battle.

Where it used to sit down the way there's now the Dove Family Bible Church of Christ. It takes up about the full lot, and it's way more packed than the store ever was. This is round and futuristic, like Jesus came down in a flying saucer the day of the last Blue Light Special and finally gave America the church it deserved, with day-care and Starbucks coffee and Coldstone ice cream and even a pharmacy, imagine that.

I knew there would be trouble as soon as they started building this monstrosity, but the way I figured, who that could ever be saved would fall for such a bullshit bastardization of the gospel? I thought the competition would make me a better minister. What brings out the best in a man more than something looming?

As we cruise the lot, I look at the cars gathering as the sun goes down. No one can see in the triple tinted windows. I recognize a few of the folks getting out of their cars. They dressed up for this one. No more plaid shirts and blue jeans and t-shirts. It's all dresses and suits and some even brought shiny bags with them, full of tithe and whatever else. Maybe ol' Reverend Lonnie finally decided to put Walmart out of business once and for all, and put in a little mall.

I don't hold anything against the fuckers who built it or the sheep milling their way toward the entrance. I don't wish death on my fellow man like that. But I just have to see. I have to know what's inside that's so great, it would tear them away from me the way it did.

The venom courses through my veins. I get out of Garth's hatchback. I feel like I could tear all the purple out of the sky and collect it and make something from it, a flower maybe, or that dude on the McDonald's bags.

The asphalt sizzles. Nothing but eggs raining from the sky and when they hit the yolk immediately curdles up. Everyone waving at their faces like a bunch of lonely cows trekked through hell.

Focus.

The façade of the church is clean and pretty. I'll give

them that much. I never understood buildings that moved at angles like an alien's costume on a '60s TV show. Brick or log, four walls, that's all I need. Seems like a good way to impress people is to just keep adding walls. The idea probably started with the Pentagon. *We've got five walls,* they said. *One more than necessary. There's some important shit going on here.*

The poison flows through me and all I can focus on are the patterns on the dresses of the women going inside. There's a pastel blue where sunflowers swim and something like a representation of the whole universe, a fractal pattern of shine and glitter. Another dress looks like it'd feel like a potato sack, and for a moment I'm thinking about mud-covered heathens in potato sacks in some soupy courtyard back in the time of knights and dragons, and they're wondering why God left them there, at that point in life, and then god tells them there's more lives than the one they're living, and that they should look forward to the time that they're a man in a parking lot with snake venom coursing through his veins, a gun at his neck, thinking about what he might do.

Focus.

Lonnie Dove and his big stupid teeth, like if you tried to turn the assistant sales manager at a Hummer dealership into an underwear model. No one in town was fooled by the phony name, but they ate it up nonetheless. His real name was Lonnie Cargill, and he had long since cut ties with his Alabama Piney Woods background, somehow made his genuine folksy mannerisms feel like a robot taught them to him. Took his whole grift straight from those prosperity gospel books. There he is, standing at the doorway of the church, shaking every callused hand that comes through with palms softer than a baby's tongue. Look at the bushes. They have a gift for the topiary. Focus. He's tall, too tall, head almost grazing the top of the doorway, and his hair is a black oil wave we could drown in.

I stand in line with the rest of the sheep. Feels as unnatural to me as a shepherd chewing grass. But I stand, and I wait.

Just short of shaking the shepherd's hand, Garth steers me out of line and ushers me into one of those booths they used to have in theaters for parents with screaming children. A couple folks with no babies but who probably felt under-dressed for this church turn to look, and get up and shuffle out under Garth's scowling invitation to beat feet.

There's a band and a choir. They're pretty good, but no spirituals, just the Christian pop shit that sounds like a boy who needs a cold shower getting the wrong ideas about Jesus. I pop a couple of the 160 mg Oxys, sucking determinedly at the time-release coating until it wears off and the bare medicine turns my tongue into wood. I swallow them both, and I don't feel it, but I find myself hating the music less and less.

And the whole time, Garth is on his phone, and he's showing me this and showing me that. "See man, what people don't really get is, we're not fucking Nazis, you know? I mean. Just…whatever you say we are, that's what we are. We didn't care about this shit until they made a deal out of it. I go on these sites, look, here's fucking CNN, and they're talking about Pepe and they're talking about the 'alt-right' and all this shit. You know what this shit was, before Trump was president? It was called 'the fucking internet.' It's always been there. It's that thing that everyone is a part of, but no one wants to admit. Look at this:"

He shows me a bunch of moving images, not video, but moving images, repeated ad nauseum. In each video, a woman is being pummeled by a set of fists.

"You can see shit like this," Garth scrolls a bit. The Christian boy band keeps their shit up. The singer gyrates a bit. "But then you can also see this:"

He scrolls again, and it's pictures of dogs. That's it. Just dogs. Puppies.

The booth feels small, suffocating. I don't know what he's talking about. I don't really care.

"This has always been a place for us to be us, you know? It's a place where we don't have to worry about being fucking judged. It's a place where, you know, humor is important."

"Garth," I say, "I don't care."

He stares at me, those empty blue Aryan eyes, and his muscles tense. "Then don't call me a fucking Nazi. Cuck."

"But…"

"But nothing, gay boy. The frog isn't fucking Nazi. The frog is Kek. You know Kek? It's like, a chaos god. We're all about the frog. We're like, uh, have you seen *The Dark Knight?*"

The walls of the booth are beginning to squeeze. The boy band has finished their song. Blondes rush the stage, and that's all I can see, the singer kneeling down to touch each of their hands, and through the glass I can hear them. It sounds like hell. I close my eyes and let myself tumble down into the pit.

I must be nodding off, because Garth knocks my head into the glass to wake me up when Reverend Lonnie Dove finally comes out.

He smiles at the audience like he just bought those teeth with their money. Then he hunches his shoulders a bit, seems to kind of shrink, somehow, artfully, to become One Of Us.

Garth mercifully goes back to his phone. His breathing intensifies as soon as the screen lights up.

Lonnie starts his line: "Friends… I read about this

doctor at a big university up north," he says, "and this fella said he'd discovered a part of the brain that is responsible for us believing in God. That we're wired for faith, the same way your house is wired for electricity… Those atheist folks always think they have the answers, don't they?"

Half of Lonnie's parishioners are shaking their heads. The other half seem to wake up thinking they're at a WWE cage match. All of a sudden those blondes look ready to put those well-manicured fingernails through somebody's eyes.

"You know how folks who almost died on the operating table or a car crash are always saying they saw the tunnel with all their ancestors in it, and the light of Heaven at the end… The ones who saw the other place aren't so quick to call up the *Enquirer*, I suppose… Well, this fellow, he claimed he could make you see the pearly gates, the fires of Hell or UFO aliens taking you up in their saucer, just by tickling the temporal lobes of your brain. And he said this proved that God was just a thing in our heads we're programmed to believe in, His voice like a ventriloquist's dummy telling us what we won't want to hear, when we can't see any other way out but giving up."

Some in the crowd shout out, "NO!" and some nastier things, but even those who are riled up seem to enjoy it. Garth says, "Dude, you have to see this," and

I tell him to please shut the fuck up.

Lonnie: "Well folks, my family was awful sore about having their vacation plans changed up at the last minute, but… well… I went up there…"

He has to pause and smile for a while to let the crowd cheer. Then he says, "Yes, I surely did. And I tried his little machine… and you know what? It worked. I saw the pearly gates and Saint Peter and Jesus and my Momma and a whole mess of lost family and friends, just like I always pictured it."

The crowd is silent.

"And I wept, I'm not ashamed to say. And that fella, he was sitting there with a big ol' grin like a cat with a mouthful of mouse, waiting for me to cry uncle and say I'd seen the light… and I told him straight out that I wanted to thank him for proving to the world once and for all that He is REAL…"

The crowd goes wild.

"He is ALIVE…"

Louder.

"And we are LOVED."

Their souls come out their mouths for screaming.

He waits for them to settle down with a patient smirk. "And the fellow looked at me like I was crazy, I won't lie. But if you find a radio and hear a voice at the other end, you just got to know somebody made that radio so they could talk to you. Somebody put that radio in your head so you would receive His message. I don't see how even a couple billion years of evolution would come up with something like that, how just dumb blind luck would create a radio that would tell you lies about the Lord. But for one for whom the whole universe is just a little bitty garden, for one to whom an eon is but a day, who could snap His fingers and shut down the whole show or turn it on its head, a little radio inside the head of every little soul in creation would be a mighty clever idea.

"Now, I know another scientific fellow who is also a devoted believer, who told me once that for God, if he is truly singular and alone above of all that is, then all of this must exist as a dream, an idea—he called it a hologram—in the mind of the Lord, all to be swept away the moment He decided it was time for dinner."

Garth says, "Speaking of dinner, look at what this guy is fucking *eating*."

I once again ask him to shut the fuck up.

Lonnie: "So some say He's just a notion in our heads, and some say we're all just a little spark of an idea in His. But WE know the truth in our hearts and our souls, don't we?"

The audience shouts out how right their hearts are.

"How clever is our God?"

The crowd roars in approval of their God's cleverness.

"How AWESOME is our God?"

The audience tears its throat out proclaiming the awesomeness of their god.

They're locusts, their shrill chittering cries come from stropping their legs against their abdomens.

Garth says, "His sermons are better than yours. Not trying to be a dick, but, you know."

I turn to him. The pills have my world straight. I say, "Thank you, Garth."

After the sermon, Garth and a goon lead me to an elevator that takes a password to open. They lead me down a hallway with carpet on the ceiling and walls as well as the floor, thirsty walls that swallow sound. A cart with a bell cover on it like from fancy hotel room service sits outside a room. Garth knocks and when he hears a noise inside, he pushes me into a mostly blank space with a big desk.

Lonnie Cargill sits poring over two computers and a laptop and popping blackheads on the end of his nose. Without looking up, he smiles and waves at a handsome calfskin seat comfortable enough to die in.

"There's a dinner out there," Garth says, clearly torn between telling and leaving it.

Lonnie looks up from the computers, folds his hands calmly. Blinking human eyes under all that serenity. "Well don't just sit there. Bring it in. Bless your heart, Garth, you lack the sense God gave a hookworm."

Garth goes out and comes back pushing the cart across the big but plain office, around a vast plain of a desk to park it beside the shepherd.

Lonnie starts to tuck a napkin into his shirt, then notices something. "Where's the fucking silverware, Garth?"

"I'm not a waiter, Lonnie. I'm a consultant."

That hangs there for a beat. The Reverend looks to be steadying his breath. Carefully: "Watch your mouth. And go get me some goddamn silverware."

Garth reluctantly heads out, looking at me and taking comfort in the notion I present no real threat.

Lonnie leans back in his chair and steeples his long pianist's fingers, tilts his chin in the direction of my arm. "You know, you ought to get that looked at."

The black necrosis spreads out from under the bandage. What with the unchecked destruction of tissues owing to the hemotoxins in the venom, the rest of my hand has the color and texture of an overripe tomato. "The Lord knows what I'm going through."

"Maybe you'd like me to pray over it for you."

"If God wants to call me home, I suppose he will."

"Clyde, we both know the Good Lord would've struck you dead a long time ago, if He could…" He clicks his tongue, pantomiming switching gears. Thumps his fingers on the desk. "I know this fella, just moved down to this part of the country from DC, and he's real proud of his yard, right? Ain't no country boy, but he likes to work the earth, so when he bought this new place with real pretty flowering trees all around it, he was ecstatic, but then when he settled in and started looking closer, he found a mess of parasitic creepers were strangling the trees. Big ugly vines like snakes all twined round the branches, like hiding in amongst 'em. So he took a shovel and some pruning shears, and he went to town, digging up root and branch and ripping them creepers out the trees, and you know what he found, when he was done?"

I shrug and something cracks in my back.

"He found, that all those pretty flowers and leaves were from the vines, and all the trees were long dead— just a bunch of rotten old wood that crumbled away when he ripped out all them nasty vines."

He rolls open a drawer on his desk and removes a pinewood box. He opens it and sets a baggie of speed out on the pristine surface of the desk. He carefully opens it as he talks:

"What I'm saying is, you and I know they killed all the trees around here long ago, cut 'em down or leached the soil until their roots just curled up and starved to death standing up. Ain't nothin' left round here but us parasitic creepers, Clyde. You ain't no tree, and you sure as shit ain't no gardener."

He spills the powder and chops up a huge speed

bump of white crystals and snorts it, offers me some, laughs at my disgusted expression. "Not what you think. Top of the line smart drugs from Sandoz Labs. You know they invented LSD? You know what that is? Never mind, anyway… Dopamine, for optimized neurochemical function, and a blast of vasopressin right before I go on, for bushier, more oxygenated dendrites… that's why I never need to write my shit down anymore, I just kick it from my heart." He beats his chest and shouts, "WOO!"

He treats his other nostril to a spray of the aforementioned dendrite from a black plastic atomizer and sits back, growling in his throat. "You heard my sermon, right? I believe that, I truly do." Sniff. "God is just that little voice in your head that tells you what you won't hear. And what is that little voice telling you, Clyde? To take up snakes and drink poison to prove your faith, because you can't swallow your pride and admit even your God wants you gone off the earth?"

At this point, I just stare.

"And what did you do when vipers and poison couldn't do the job? You took up human snakes and spread their venom, but you didn't become one of them. You wanted to be something worse. You thought you'd stay righteous right up until the day they bit you and killed you dead, and the other po' folk would say there was a man who turned evil to good… a goddamn redneck Robin Hood."

Lonnie pushes his chair back and stands. He does a few jumping jacks. Reaches back absently for the chair, pulls it under him. Adjusts his tie. Breathes.

"Difference between you and me is, I don't hate myself for being what I am, or God for making me so. I'm playing this game to win, because that's what my God loves. Winners, Clyde. Not martyrs.

"But," he concludes with a deep, theatrical sigh, "every once in a sweet while, God lets everyone get what they want, and I reckon this'll be one of those times."

He takes out a pair of reading glasses and an iPad and scrolls through a list. "So let's see… From our investment of seventy-two K, you in turn put a good sum into expanding your operation, which has since gone up in smoke. Ditto your retail arm, in that lamentable unpleasantness at the Walmart. You're sitting on a large inventory you can no longer move, and your supplier has stiffed you on stock that you can, hence your inability to make good on our dividends. Am I missing anything?"

I give it some thought. "No, that's about right."

"Well, good we're on the same page. Do I wish it could've gone smoother? Sure. Garth said you'd had a change of heart after your brush with mortality, there, and your stepping out would've been just the right grace note. But some folks just can't lie down and the let the world go on, can't stand the thought of it, gotta try to burn it all down in their wake, like a selfish child with a sandcastle."

I don't have anything for that.

"You thought you were doing these folks good, the lesser of two evils. That's why we bought in, because you were doing it for all the wrong reasons, and bound to crack up sooner or later. You won't sell heroin and such to your hillbilly cousins, so I guess you'll still get into heaven, right?"

His chin dips all the way down to his desk, then slurps back up to normal. I shake my head, and his eyes are two sizes too big, like some kind of cartoon.

"Credit where it's due, you came up with the scam, and I'm thankful. No better front than a church. The tax folks and the cops are petrified to mess with the Lord's house. One reason I chose this path over politics."

I look up to the walls and it's a million squirming earthworms and they pile up on top of each other until the wall is almost crushing us. Then it snaps into place.

"But you were too small, and didn't try until way too late to get big. You're too righteous to do the work, and too weak to do the necessary. No wonder the Mexicans are eating your lunch. You're fucking up everything for everybody, Clyde."

I look down at my hand, and it's not some fucked-up claw anymore. It's a metal fist, a robot fist, and it's glowing with fire.

"But as per usual, I got the answer." Lonnie puts down the iPad and picks up an empty gym bag with MAKE AMERICA PRAY AGAIN! emblazoned across it and tosses it at Garth. "Get twenty out of the plate and take it down there."

Garth can't help it. He checks his phone quick. "To who?"

"To Angel Salcido, dipshit. Tell him it's a good faith offering, but we'd like to take delivery of the good preacher's heroin shipment, and request an audience to consider our mutual responsibilities."

My hand still glows. I need to go home. "You sit down with the cartel, they're gonna be eating more than your lunch."

"Listen to Scarface, here."

Garth spins his phone. "I don't wanna go down there... I don't speak fucking Spanish. Let Dale and Gunther do it."

"I don't care if you send it with a fucking drone. Just don't fuck it up."

The whole room glows, then it doesn't. A slow strobe. I say, "You've got nothing to offer them but your ass."

"Clyde, you've been listening to too much hysterical talk radio." He laughs at his joke a little too long, until we all remember how he has a radio show, see what he did there? "But seriously, these boys know drugs, but they don't know this part of the country too well at all, and they don't blend."

"That's a fact."

Lonnie just smiles. "Like I said, no better front than a church. These folks won't buy balloons of black tar spit out by some strange beaner in an old beat-up car. If he'll supply us and stay quiet, we can get him protection all the way to the top. If he don't want a war, he'll know we can do a lot for each other."

"I wish you every happiness in your new blessed union."

"I don't grok this bullshit," Garth grumbles from the door.

Lonnie slams his hand on the desk. "Why're you still here?"

"What'm I supposed to do with the preacher?"

"Take him home. If he'll give up the inventory and the rest of our money, let him go die in his bed."

"What if he doesn't?"

"He will."

"No I won't."

"Aw hell, Clyde. Nobody wants a mess."

"What if he won't?"

"I don't give a shit. Take him to Sunday School."

14

The sign on the door does indeed say "SUNDAY SCHOOL." Garth and his friend Gunther have to practically carry me like a bride over the threshold.

Gunther is the kind of fellow every group with flagging self-esteem needs at its center—a tubby, four-fingered dupe with a kicked-puppy expression on his unlined moon pie face. He takes the bag from Garth and stands there until Garth feeds him Lonnie's instructions like a mama bird regurgitating worms for a big dumb babybird.

"What about this guy?" He points at me.

"He wouldn't fit in the lost and found bin."

Gunther looks at me and giggles. He can't take his eyes off me now.

The walls are adorned with weapons and military regalia—Confederate and Nazi, mostly, with a few weapons on display, more for their badness than for historical authenticity, like ninja throwing stars, nunchuks and a couple of spears next to a Spartan warrior's helmet and a big flag that says MOLON LABE on it.

Garth makes himself at home in their little honeycomb hideout. Two other pasty fellows with whitewall haircuts sprawl on a couch, watching a revolting cartoon on a big flatscreen that can't possibly be for kids.

Maybe it comes of a life spent forbidden to—and then forbidding others to—watch television, but I never could follow why grown men would watch cartoons. Pornography, I understand well enough, but these boys are watching a cartoon where a girl is raped by some sort of a demon, but he doesn't even have an honest cock and balls. Tentacles with eyes and teeth come slithering out of him as he laughs at her, pinning her and twisting her nipples, throbbing and pumping lord-knows-what into her until she half comes to enjoy it.

I wonder how these Aryan boys come to enjoy this Asian shit.

I think to myself that maybe I was too harsh on the ol' one-eyed devil. And then as I look at these boys, I see this isn't even porn for them, it's just another cartoon. One of them is holding a pillow the size of a person with a girl's picture on it, texting on a phone as he watches. Somehow, they've come to this, without losing their innocence. This is the master race. They don't even know what death is, and they're gonna try to sell it.

Which is what strikes me funny, when I go about my business of killing Garth and his friends.

Gunther sees my sick hand coming up out of its sling, but doesn't register the fork I pocketed from Lonnie's supper until it's sticking out of his neck.

I don't know if you've ever chanced to stick a fork in one of us, but it's harder than it looks. He may look like he's made out of meringue and bad decisions, but Gunther's a thick boy. The tines barely break his skin, and I damn near lose the fork as he steps back. His natural gunslinger reflexes kick in and he pistol-whips me across the face hard enough to knock me down, then the gun goes off into the ceiling and a light fixture falls on their custom felted poker table.

"Put the safety on, fatass." Garth jumps up and comes over to slap Gunther across the face and kick me in the ribs. "We were gonna be nice to you, old man. Let you tell us where that shit is. We thought we might even let you live."

Gunther is moaning that he's bleeding to death. His friends tell him to shut the fuck up.

"But that shit has sailed," Garth says. "Suck on this." He kicks me again and two ribs give way. One may or may not have punched a hole in my lung. I roll with it, closer to Gunther. When Gunther goes to kick me again, I twist away, nearly fainting with the pain, and stab him in the foot with the stolen steak knife.

The knife goes through the cheap leather of Gunther's steel-toed stormtrooper boot, through skin, tendons and skin again, then the sole of the boot, the carpet and subfloor. Gunther jerks backward so the knife tugs on his foot, pinned like a bug. He goes crosseyed with the pain, emitting a high canine whine.

I lever up on the knife and drive the fork into Gunther's crotch, just to the side of his woefully shrunken tackle and into that big artery up in there, using my sick hand, little more than a meat puppet swollen shut around the handle. The impact drives a gusher of dead black blood into my veins and silver snakes swim across my eyes. *Now*, you're bleeding to death, I want to tell him. He falls on me. Garth shoots at me and hits Gunther twice. I feel one punch into my belly after coming through the big boy, who twists and writhes, squealing on top of me, catching three more shots from his friends.

I squirm out from under him and pick up Gunther's gun, point it and remember to flip off the safety. Garth has taken cover behind the bar, the other two behind the couch. Nothing really hurts, I just wish they'd stop shooting…

A hell of a thing, Lord. This piece of metal gets me in the shoulder, it's a little diamond-shaped disk with the edges sharpened. One on the couch screams at his friend, "See, I fucking told you!" As he goes for the rest of the throwing stars in the display, I shoot him in the head and chest. His friend clutches the pillow over his chest, forcing me to shoot him through it, which makes me feel pretty terrible. These big cartoon titties exploding, his blood coming out the back end.

Then Garth shoots at me from behind the bar. My gun is empty, so I throw it at him. It hits the tiered display of hard alcohol bottles behind him, shattering the glass shelves so they come down on his head. He screams and curses, "Goddamn bandwidth!" and his gun goes off once.

I force myself to my feet, dimly aware of a whirring like a huge fan at my back. Somewhere, I hear music. Choir practice? No, the girl in the Japanese demon-rape cartoon has turned into a bigger demon, a vagina demon. I stagger over to the wall and grab the nearest harmful-looking object and circle behind the bar. It's one of those old-timey German helmets with the big spike on top.

Perfect.

Garth is struggling against the bar, angrily trying to access one last Scheizeporn video on his phone, but there's blood from a massive gash on his forehead all over his hands, the screen a smeary mess.

He looks up at me and spits blood. I turn the helmet over and drive the spike into the crown of Garth's skull. He gags and sputters and chokes out, "YOU… FUCKING… CUCK."

Truer words were never said, I think, but I just tell him, "Suck on that," and watch close as his eyes go flat. I lose count of Mississippis between heartbeats. In the distance, I hear a noise like soft mallets on a steel drum.

It's Garth's phone, there on the floor. I pick it up and wipe away the blood and look down at the screen. It's one of his drones, and that's when I notice the gigantic, angry dragonfly hovering behind me.

It floats before me, props chewing air and cameras tracking my movement and an array of little bottle-rocket missiles and a little nozzle attached to a jury-rigged flamethrower peeking out from its underbelly.

I wipe Garth's blood off the phone. A grainy image of a dying old man stares out at me, then looks at the phone in his hand. Two options appear on the screen: *Execute* and *Cancel*. I hit *Cancel*. The screen takes me to a map of the county, and I feel my heart begin to race. I zoom in on Elizabeth. Then I zoom in closer, on the church that used to be a K-Mart.

Technology is a real miracle. I can see the church there, plain as day. I zoom in further, just little reverse-pinches of my fingers, and there it is: The Dove Bible

Church. I double-tap the screen. Again, that same message: *Execute* or *Cancel*.

I never got the appeal of videogames, either. Daddy condemned them as a worse sin than gambling. But I've seen enough of them being played to nudge Garth's toy killing machine out the door of the Sunday School room and into the carpeted corridor down the way from the main auditorium, where the boy band is still harmonizing and the janitors are mopping up discarded crutches and spilt love offerings out of the pews, I reckon.

I send the drone down the hall in the direction of that boy band and when I can see a fire exit at the end of the hall, I click "Execute."

Out in the parking lot, everybody's running to watch the fire, screaming in tongues, drunk on the carnage like it's hillbilly Mardi Gras. The big football game, then the massacre at the Walmart, and now this little miracle.

But there's still much to be done.

My chest feels like the back end of a thunderstorm. If I stop to catch my breath, I'll stop breathing. Pop another Oxy, try to manipulate Garth's keys, phone and the gym bag, limping away from a burning church with Angel's words rattling around in my head.

Was I asking for this?

Maybe, so, maybe no.

15

Driving back to Palestine in Garth's hatchback, I call Donna on Garth's phone. She picks up right away.

"Clyde, where you been, I been trying to call you…"

"It's alright, honey… I had to go see to some things, but I'm coming back, and I… I got something for you. I need you to keep it, and get out of town, and maybe… do something good with it somewhere…"

"That's real good, Clyde, but I need you to come here with it. They won't hurt me, if you come right over…"

I can't hear what she says after that, but I know where to go. Her words are scoured away by the scream of a racing machine held up to the phone.

A belt sander.

I clutch at my gut when they hang up. I can feel the nugget of lead in the muscle of my belly, not too deep under the hole. Maybe they'll let Donna dig it out of me. Maybe she'll do it after they let us go.

Maybe they will, I tell myself. Maybe enough people have died for no reason today. Maybe we'll go down south and open a heroin treatment clinic and scrub these stains out of our dirty, worthless souls.

It's not too much to hope for, on a day like today. I was supposed to die this morning, so everything since then has been pure gravy.

Angel Salcido is kneeling before one of the display alcoves in the Halloween Store when two masked hoods bring me to him. Candles, fetishes, bowls of drugs, gold, bones and blood at the feet of a real human skeleton in black robes with a blacklight halo. He takes a joint fat as a Cuban cigar, rolls the massive orange ember into a bowl of cocaine, sucks reverently and blows the smoke into her face, whispering a wordless prayer.

When his rush dissipates, he asks me if I'd like to make an offering to Santa Muerte.

I politely decline.

"You're in bad shape, boss," he says. "You should cover all your bases, you know, regardless. You go round like it don't matter what you do, so long as you love Jesus. But right now, it don't look like nobody up there loves you back. Get right with what's coming, padre."

I ask him where Donna is.

He smiles, amused by my disrespect. "I want to show you something first, so we understand each other."

As respectfully as he can, he shunts Santa Muerte aside and pulls back the black lacy curtains of the shrine to show where they've knocked out a doorway in the wall. "Come look," he says.

I follow him through the hole into the dark shell of the old Rexall Drug. It changed names half a dozen times before it went belly up last year, and aside from a couple suicides and overdoses on the premises, nobody's had cause to piss on it since. But the Mexicans have swept up the spent condoms and beer bottle glass and set up something behind walls of clear plastic. Inside, a couple folks in rubber suits like they wear for germ warfare experiments work on a little assembly line.

"No shit, spared no expense, jefe. Down to the stamp, perfect pharmaceutical counterfeits, but stronger. Way fucking stronger. We're not just competing with other cartels no more. Drug companies cut in on our turf, but we're Mexicans, padre. Doing more, harder, faster for cheaper is how we always bury you. We're looking at turning out ten thousand pills a day here by Thanksgiving."

The men in suits are gargoyles sitting on the roof of a church watching an assembly of birds roll by. I think of Donna and I keep myself in check. I say, "Don't matter if you put me in the ground. Nobody in this county will take your pills, Angel."

His big sad face strains for a frown. "I know, they feel better buying weak-ass oxycodone from their minister, but we got a new partner who will front for us."

One of the hooded workers looks at me furtively and spends a long time pouring freshly minted pills into a row of funnels, with his back to me. One of his hands is splinted, like somebody slammed it in a door.

"That's all we want, padre. We don't want to hurt you and get off on the wrong foot, here. Just give up. Stick to preaching and stop playing with snakes."

"Angel," I say, "don't you come from a small town like this?"

He shrugs and nods. "Even smaller. No phone or electricity in my town, until you good people made it possible."

"They know what you are? What you do? Are they proud of you?"

"Hell yes, they are. Where I come from, drug dealers are lower than pimps. But we don't sell our shit to each other. We watch, we learn. We were businessmen, but you're always the ones saying this is a war, right? When I come home, I will buy a new soccer stadium and a park for my home town, and they will know I am a fucking warrior."

Angel leads me back through the hole in the wall to the showroom, then through the bead curtain into the stockroom.

Donna sits at a table in the employee breakroom, smoking a cigarette. Hector Basilone sits opposite her, wearing a big black Stetson and a clean green surgical mask. The Makita belt sander sits on the table between them, the cord snaking back to a socket in the wall above the sink.

Blood dapples the filter from her fat lip. "Hey, Clyde."

"Donna…"

"You didn't bring it," she says. Her eyes go wide and wild. "Why didn't you bring it?"

I don't try to tell her what this town will turn into, once it's a wholly owned franchise of the Sinaloa Cartel and the megachurch down the road. I tell her we're both going to die, anyway, it's just a question of how big a mess we force them to make.

Angel puts a hand on my shoulder. "We don't want to hurt you, padre, but we're serious, here. We want the money and the drugs. Put it in my hand, and we'll take you both home, or to a motel, you know, regardless."

Donna stifles a sob and stabs out the cigarette.

"But even if you don't give a shit about her, we'll have no choice but to search the church, your house, you know…"

"Regardless," I finish for him.

He smiles and cuffs me across the face with his gold-plated automatic. "We don't want to hurt nobody."

I smile and try to spit out blood, but it just dribbles down my chin. "I deserve to be hurt."

Angel nods, pleased with the truth. "Sure you do. But does she?"

Donna whips her head around and her face is a permafrost mask. "Just give it to them, Clyde, god damn you…"

Angel punches me in the gut, bending me over his arm, and throws me into the employee restroom like a bundle of dirty laundry.

The door slams and I trip over the toilet. The light switch doesn't bring light. Fumbling around, all I can find is a toilet plunger, a can of cleanser, an air freshener and the sink.

Lord, I know I've offended you more than a time or two, but so was I made, and no better. But I like to think I might surprise you once or twice, or why make me at all?

I turn on both the taps and the plumbing groans, and then I can't hear anything for the duet of the belt sander and my mistress on the other side of the door.

Most of the quality folks in these parts drink tank water or bottled, but they'll swear there's nothing wrong with the tap. And the mining company that fracks under our feet says there's nothing unnatural about tapwater you can set on fire. The water only trickles out, even after I kick the fixtures out of the wall, but the sweet fecal reek of methane gushes out the pipes to fill the room.

My head is swimming. The belt sander roars. Donna shrieks like an air raid siren, a long, breathless, agonized rendition of my name.

I grab the toilet plunger, snap the rubber end off under the toilet seat, lay down on the floor and kick the door, screaming, *"Let me out, you cocksuckers, I'll tell you, I'll tell you where it is!"*

The belt sander falls silent. Donna sobs. The door opens. Angel steps into the dark restroom with the joint in his mouth. "What the fuck you been eating, padre—"

The cloud of methane explodes in Angel's face. Like a bullwhip cracking from here to Florida. He staggers into the doorframe with his hair on fire.

I barely covered my eyes, and I'm still half-blind, but I roll upright and drive the shaft of the toilet plunger into Angel's crotch.

Hector guns the belt sander and comes running at me. Hot blood gushes over my hands. Blind and badly burned, Angel sits down hard, batting at his blazing hair as his life gushes down his leg. I fight my way to my feet and grab the doorframe, fumble around the corner for the lightswitch, flick it.

The breakroom plunges into blackness.

The belt sander falls silent.

Hector curses and drops it on the table.

I fall onto Angel and try to pry the automatic out of his hand, but he's laying on it. Just the flashes of flame to light the dark.

Hector shoots blind. The muzzle flashes show me he's down against the water cooler across the breakroom. Donna clings to the floor.

I try to roll Angel over. Hector shoots again and puts one into my back. Angel rolls over and I roll with him. Lever up on one elbow and grab for the breakroom counter. Hector reloads.

I hit the lightswitch. The belt sander fires up and charges across the table like a vicious little dog and leaps at Hector's face. The racing sandpaper belt catches him on the jaw and gypsum teeth rip into his cheek before he bats it away, crashing into the watercooler.

Angel's automatic is a goddamn cannon. It's all I can do to lift it up in my good hand. My first shot hits the cooler and shatters the plastic so a wave of soothing water splashes over Hector just before I put five bullets in his face and chest.

I drag myself over to Donna. She's shaking, and in spite of everything, I almost believe her.

"Your talents were wasted here," I tell her. "You really should've gone on to Hollywood, instead of staying here with me."

She squints at me. Reaches into her pocket, pulls out a pack of cigarettes. Lights one. "Nobody can fool you but yourself, I suppose."

"I was gonna give it to you," I said.

"Thanks for that," she said. "I never wanted it. I just wanted to have something for me, instead of always being the fucking side dish." As she looks around, I can read in her sulking features how these men I just killed were all the hope she had. Turn the urgent care clinic into another pill mill, sell Angel's heroin to chronic pain and disability cases, which amounts to half the town.

"You can still get more than any of us will ever get," I tell her, pointing the gun at her. "You can get *out*."

She looks around, then turns to the door as someone on the other side says in a hushed voice, "*Carnal? Que pasa?*"

I shoot twice through the door.

Shaking like the DT's, Donna climbs to her feet. For just a moment, her eyes alight on Hector's pistol, then she grabs her purse off the counter and leaves without another word, stepping over the mess in the hallway just before Angel's phone rings.

I feel about an inch thick, and fit to blow away on

the next breeze. Every breath takes an act of will. I pick it up and look at the local number on the screen.

"Hey, Sheriff."

"Hey, uh… Clyde…?"

"You got the right number, Early. Angel's in the toilet. You want to leave a message?"

"Thought you were fixin' to die when I left you this afternoon. I'd hoped you'd be a bit more discreet in seeing to your affairs, but since I got you on the phone…"

"I won't lie to you, Early. I gave a fair chunk of it to the Mexicans for drugs, and they stiffed me, as I'm sure you know. The rest appears to have gone missing, and the first person I suspected, to be perfectly honest, is you."

He clicks his tongue and I can hear his jowls lift off his teeth in a big shit-eating grin. "You're a right clever detective when you wanna be, only the way I'll tell it is, I came across your truck parked behind your little chapel, when I was called upon to investigate the fire… such a goddamn tragedy for a town to lose *two* churches in one day…"

"God damn you, Early Ramage…"

He cackles. "So sad, to think someone might be harboring a terrible grudge against you and yours… But real lucky I happened to find that suitcase in your truck. I was just going to tell our friend Angel he didn't need to mess with you no more, but now… well, I'd hate to lie to a preacher… I don't know quite what to do."

"Why don't you just come on over here, and we'll pray on it."

16

"Trick or treat," Early says as he comes in the door, "smell my feet…"

I'm sitting behind the counter opposite the door, in front of a big display of Halloween masks, so Early doesn't recognize me from the other rubber monsters until I start talking.

"You done got every last treat I had, Sheriff."

He looks over at me in the dark store, at the big golden gun on the counter in front of me, and knows I couldn't pick it up right now with a forklift. "I wouldn't put it past you to have a trick or two up your sleeve, Clyde." He ambles over with his pistol in one hand and the briefcase in the other. "Was a hell of a mess up at the Walmart, I tell you what. Seven folks dead for no reason, and them no-good Gunns. You did me a big ol' favor there, I won't lie. Offically we called it a robbery, and it'll most likely stick. But that mess up at the church. I suppose you think you raised hell."

"We all made this place the hell that it is."

"And you thought you'd make it right by tearing it down in a day. Hell, I can understand you trying to get right with the Lord, but if you think you cut off the head, boy, you sure wasted your last day on earth. All you done was give us a harsh haircut, son. It looks bad now, but it'll grow out and no one will ever speak of it again."

He leans forward, warming to the subject. Today, everybody wants to preach to the preacher. "Because we all know this shitty little rigged game is as close as we'll ever get to heaven. It only gets worse, and you used to know it. The preacher up in Elizabeth, he knows what people need. You used to keep 'em in line, too, until the spirit moved you to fuck it all up. You didn't leave us no damn choice, Clyde."

"I sold false hope in one hand and poison in the other until I didn't know the difference."

"Ain't no difference worth takin' notice of." His big stubby fingers drum the side of the briefcase.

"So what do you need me for? You got everything you wanted."

"Drugs would've been nice, but we'll find those, if they ain't burned up. Shame about that fire, and I don't suppose your reputation will survive you by much. Still, nobody expected much better out of you Hilburns… Them holy rollers who crack the whip hardest always need the most whippin'."

"Early, are you fixing to talk me to death?"

"Where are my manners?" He pushes the briefcase towards me. "I think we can close this case without dragging your survivors into it, soon as I can open this one. I'd hate to damage this real nice property or the contents. Is there a key for this thing, or what?"

I reach towards it with my good hand. I start to tell him I never programmed the locks, but someone has been running me all day. When the latches don't pop even when the tumblers are set to the default of 000, I try to think for a moment like I'm scheming. If the party who put me on this path reprogrammed the lock, then I suppose this is part of the message, too.

"You still awake there, Clyde?"

I realize my eyes are pinching shut, and I can feel very little beyond the frostbite tingle in my fingers. I fumble the numbers on the left latch to 1-6-1, and the ones on the right to 7-1-8.

The latches pop open. I start to open it, thinking of the look on Garth's face when he saw the crazy cache of snakeskin and mining scrip. *A hillbilly declaration of war…*

Early pins my hand to the briefcase and points the pistol at me. "Thank you kindly, Clyde," he says, and shoots me in the chest.

A little left of center, but it punches right through my lung and out my back so clean I feel the chill of the cavity through me. I fall back against the display wall. Severed heads of werewolves, vampires and the last several presidents tumble over me.

"I hope you get better than you deserve, Clyde," Early says. "I honestly do." He opens the briefcase and his big ruddy face puckers like a fist just before the rattler strikes.

The fangs go into the right eyelid and the fleshy bulb of Early's nose. He screams like a trapped rabbit. Staggering backwards, he grabs the dangling snake and yanks so hard that the fang in his nose breaks off and his eye comes halfway out of its socket with the other. His face bloats up and blackens, the ruin of his right eye squirting out like the yolk of an egg.

He bullwhips the rattlesnake on the counter and flings it away. His legs describe a crazy squaredance as he howls my name and shoots at whatever he sees through the venom and blood gushing out his eye.

Finally, he fetches up against the counter and points the gun into the face of a Jimmy Carter mask. "You devil," he says, and blasts it. Styrofoam confetti flies in his half-melted face, which cracks and spits bloody pus like a sausage on the grill. "Where'd you go, you devil?"

I tell him I'm right here, but by then, he can't hear me. He sinks to the floor and kicks around in circles for a while before finally winding down, his big shoes and hairy hands the last to get the message.

By and by, I try to pull myself up to the counter, but all I manage to do is pull the briefcase down on myself. The snakeskins and coins and pills rain down on me, and the parcel hits me in the face. I pick it up, weighing it in my ruined hand. The pain nearly puts me under, blue flames and bile rising and red foam bubbles out my mouth the first deep breath I try to take.

Death is a ledge so clear I can see it right beneath my toes. I can lie back and breathe and let it go, and I might live until someone comes to throw a few spadefuls of dirt on this mess. But I'd rather know.

I tear open the parcel with my teeth and turn it over so thirty-five thousand dollars spills out in my lap.

This whole stupid game is finally almost over.

I wonder who won.

A light shines in my eyes like sunlight seen from the bottom of a well. I reach out for it, grateful for a glimpse of the light at the end at last, even if it is just a stupid movie my brain is playing. I thank you, Lord, as an angel lifts me up off the floor and I look down at Sheriff Early Ramage Jr. and the massacre of rubber faces, and I feel cheated when I don't see my earthly remains lying there, and realize Death has fucked me over yet again.

The heavenly trumpets are the sirens of the West Virginia State Police and Elizabeth Fire Department converging on our town. The angel bearing me up to glory wears overalls and a white homespun shirt, and is bald as an egg.

17

All the best things I ever did were only in service to my own pride, I admit. But all the worst I ever did, I was only ever trying to know you.

The highest I ever felt was when I took up a snake and spread the gospel, but it was the same kind of high I felt when I took up dice or drugs or a strange lady's ass. I never felt *you*. All that I did, I never took pleasure in, because I never felt your hand, but I went on doing what I did so that you would judge me and love me as my father never could.

Huey carries me into the cabin on the mountaintop that my great-granddaddy holed up in after he was bit by a cottonmouth at a tent revival while running from the law. He lays me down on a couch and gently washes my wounds as Sally fetches me a mason jar of whiskey. When she kneels over me, the charm around her neck falls free of her patchwork coat. It's the severed rattle of a young eastern diamondback. I can't talk and she doesn't, but I can see in her eyes that in the end, I did her proud.

I cough and choke on the whiskey and there's a moment when I almost faint dead away, but Huey puts his big pale hands on me and his face creases, and I wonder what kind of meal he'll eat off my chest at the wake. I hope it'll be a four-course feast with two of Enola's best pies, to sweeten the bitterness of my sins.

When I'm steady, Huey picks me up again and carries me back through the cabin, past a blanketed palette of vacuum-sealed bundles and all the bibles, hymnals and snake-cages from the church.

My hair brushes the doorframe as we pass out into the yard, and the stars are on fire, down among the trees. I see the cloud of candlelight draw around me and the red-lit faces of my flock. Those hard-worn, haggard faces have no eyes, but in their silence, I feel the love and judgment you never spared for me.

All that I made from my business, I put into their homes, thinking I was turning the evil of other men into good. I paid their heating bills and bought Christmas presents for their children and even sent a few to college out of state, to better lives. I only spread my sin into their homes, into their lives, and they will never stop paying for it.

But we are all sineaters, up here. We still gum the rotten banquet of every lost cause since the Civil War, but we go on, for when we are cold, no one will forgive us, eat our misdeeds and set us free.

He sets me down in a lawnchair at the foot of his big copper cross. It's a cold, clear night and you can see the smoke of the church still burning down in town, and the hectic red and blue will-o-wisps round the strip mall.

I open my mouth to speak, but words fail me, as all things of this world must fail and fall away. The time for sermons is past, the empty promises of words all broken past repair. I reach down into the basket Huey sets at my feet and lift up a pure demonstration of faith.

It's a magnificent cottonmouth, nearly four feet long and eagerly hissing, fangs glistening with death. I hold the snake high and my flock begins to speak the old wordless tongue, set free from the lies in all words one last time.

The murmur of their raging faith lifts me up and I float above them with the snake draped on my right arm. It arches away and sinuously turns in the air to fix me in its gaze. Just before it strikes, I look into those golden eyes and I am born again.

I see you—

And when Paul had gathered a bundle of sticks, and laid them on the fire, there came a viper out of the heat, and fastened on his hand. And when the barbarians saw the venomous beast hang on his hand, they said among themselves, No doubt this man is a murderer, whom, though he hath escaped the sea, yet vengeance suffereth not to live. And he shook off the beast into the fire, and felt no harm. Howbeit they looked when he should have swollen, or fallen down dead suddenly: but after they had looked a great while, and saw no harm come to him, they changed their minds, and said that he was a god.

—Acts 28:1-6

CODY GOODFELLOW has written five solo novels and three more with NY Times bestselling author John Skipp. His previous collections *Silent Weapons for Quiet Wars* and *All-Monster Action* both received the Wonderland Book Award. He wrote, co-produced and scored the short Lovecraftian hygiene film *Stay At Home Dad,* which can be viewed on YouTube. As a bishop of the Esoteric Order of Dagon (San Pedro Chapter), he presides over several Cthulhu Prayer Breakfasts each year. He is also a cofounder of Perilous Press, a micropublisher of modern cosmic horror. He currenly lives in Portland, Oregon.

J DAVID OSBORNE is the author of *Black Gum* and *Low Down Death Right Easy,* and the publisher of Broken River Books. He hosts the weekly podcast *The JDO Show,* available on iTunes or your favorite podcatcher. He lives in El Paso, TX with his wife and their dog.

Instagram: @brbjdo
Twitter: @brbjdo
Podcast: thejdoshow.podbean.com

Other Releases from Broken River Books: